# CHAPTER ONE

*'No.'*

The single word was as dramatic as the way the man had stormed into Layla Woods's office and slammed a piece of paper onto her desk.

As dramatic as the man himself.

Alex Rodriguez was clearly furious. The waves of his thick, jet-black hair looked rumpled—as if he'd pushed angry fingers through it. Eyes that were nearly as dark glared down at Layla.

A long way down. Layla had to fight the urge to leap to her feet so that she could feel taller. Braver. But that would be a dead giveaway that she was rattled, wouldn't it? And she couldn't afford to let Alex know the effect he was still capable of having on her.

With a satisfyingly steady hand, she reached for the piece of paper. The memo she had sent out that morning to all the senior staff members here at the Angel Mendez Children's Hospital.

'This is the agenda for the next monthly report meeting.'

'And you've put me down as being the first presenter.' Alex folded his arms. 'The answer's no. I decline the invitation.'

'It's not an "invitation",' Layla flashed back. 'It's the case I've chosen to open the meeting. I'm sorry if it's inconvenient but it's your patient, Alex, therefore you present the case. End of story.'

The head of paediatric neurosurgery made an exasperated sound, turning as if he intended to storm out of her office in the same way he'd entered. Instead, he stopped beside the large window, with the backdrop of a bright blue October morning. Was he taking in the fabulous view of New York's Central Park that this prestigious top-floor office had to offer?

An office befitting Layla's position as the new chief of paediatrics at this famous hospital. Her dream job. A position that had been in jeopardy a few short weeks ago until Alex had stepped in to protect her.

'What the hell are you playing at, Layla?'

The angry tone of Alex's voice must have carried because Layla's secretary appeared at the open door. Layla gave her a tight smile.

'Hold my calls, please, Monica.' The tilt of her head conveyed the message that she wanted more than her calls held to deal with this. The door was tactfully closed as her secretary retreated.

'Well?' Alex turned back to face her and this time Layla got to her feet.

Slowly.

She walked to the other side of her desk but couldn't go any closer to Alex. The huge can of worms that represented their shared history was blocking the way.

Or maybe it was the memory of what had happened the first time they'd confronted each other since they'd both been working here at Angel's. When they'd been close enough for the flames of a sexual chemistry that had clearly never died completely to flare into that scorching kiss.

It couldn't happen again.

Their past had been precisely what had put her new job in jeopardy. Had she really been naïve enough to think that it had been so long ago it couldn't affect her life any more? That she could take a high-profile position like this and it wouldn't matter that she hadn't disclosed her involvement in the malpractice suit that had nearly destroyed Alex's career five years ago?

Somehow they had to move past this. Learn to work together.

'I had intended discussing the agenda with you. You declined the appointment I tried to set up last week.'

'I was busy.' Alex held her gaze. 'As you would have noticed if you'd bothered checking my electronic calendar.'

Layla kept her expression carefully neutral. She *had* checked his calendar but he could have easily suggested another time. They both knew the real truth. He had been avoiding her.

Since that kiss.

He hadn't even let her voice her thanks for the way he'd stepped in and defended her at the board meeting when her integrity had been under examination and it had been highly likely that they would decide she was not the right person to oversee the talented staff that Angel's was so proud of.

Being thwarted in expressing her appreciation had been a putdown but Layla's aggravation went deeper than that.

Good manners had been drummed into Layla Woods since she'd been knee high to a grasshopper and saying

thank you to someone who'd done her such a huge favour wasn't just about maintaining a good appearance.

It was the right thing to do.

The idea of using the monthly report meeting had
been a brainwave. OK, choosing a time she'd known
Alex was busy to offer a chance to discuss the agenda
could be deemed unprofessional, but Layla had had
enough. She was taking control.

She hadn't expected it to backfire quite so instantly.
Why hadn't Alex simply continued to avoid her? He
could have asked his deputy head of neurosurgery, Ryan
O'Doherty, to present the case on his behalf.

'It's not a current case,' Alex added. 'And it was
successful.'

Of course it was. Layla would hardly have picked a
case that was presenting a current dilemma or, worse,
one that had had a bad result.

The last thing either of them would want would be
to go over *that* old ground. To the case of the toddler,
Jamie Kirkpatrick, that had brought them together in
the first place. To the cutting-edge surgery for a complicated brain tumour that had fallen disastrously short
of being successful. Jamie had died. Alex had been sued
by a distraught family looking for someone to blame.
He'd been cleared but Layla hadn't been there to help
him celebrate, had she? She'd ended their affair the
night before Jamie's surgery.

She nodded at Alex's terse summary. 'That's precisely why I chose it. We don't just put up a current,
complicated issue to get the benefit of input from different specialties. Or to dissect what went wrong in a
case that wasn't successful. Sometimes it's a good thing
to reflect on a triumph. And Matthew *was* a triumph.'

'There are plenty of other cases you could have chosen.'

'Not one that so many people are so interested in.'

The brain tumour in the nine-year-old boy had been so rare and complicated that surgeons all over the state had refused to touch it. Until the little boy's desperate parents had brought him to Angel's as a last resort and begged Dr Rodriguez to use his legendary skills to give their son a chance to survive. And that was why it wouldn't make any difference if Ryan presented the case. Everybody already knew who the real hero was.

'The criterion for picking a case to report is that it's out of the ordinary,' Layla continued. 'From what I've heard, this one was all that everybody talked about at the time and the staff involved in the recent follow-up appointment were thrilled by Matthew's progress. I also heard that you're writing the case up for a top journal. I thought it would be nice to share that.' The occasional triumph shared at the meeting was good for everybody. A counterbalance for the heart-breaking cases.

'Shine the spotlight on someone else, Layla,' Alex growled. 'Somebody's going to wonder why you picked on me and I've been talked about more than I'm comfortable with around here lately.' Alex turned to look out of the window again as he spoke but then his gaze swerved back to Layla. 'Gossip about the Kirkpatrick case was bad enough. What happens when people start talking about the fact that I was having an affair with a married woman at the time? How do you think that's going to help my reputation?'

The glare Layla received would have intimidated anyone.

Layla straightened her spine.

'I came to Angel's for a fresh start,' Alex ground out. 'I won't allow you to drag my name through the mud.'

Oh…Lord…

OK. The plan had been to make this a public gesture of thanks, whether Alex liked it or not. She knew that this case would earn him even more respect from those colleagues who didn't know all the details of the case, even though it had been breaking news on the grapevine in the months before she'd come to Angel's. She had also known that it would be a public statement of her own faith in his abilities.

But it was a huge leap to go from not wanting her gratitude or public support to accusing her of being prepared to damage his reputation. The attack was unjustified. Unfair.

'You're not the only one who's come here for a fresh start,' Layla snapped. 'And I'm sure you haven't forgotten but I *was* the married woman. I don't want that being common knowledge any more than you do.'

'So stay away from me, then.'

Layla let out an incredulous huff. 'You're the one who came storming into *my* office.'

'Because this needed to be dealt with.'

'What needs "to be dealt with",' Layla responded, 'is the fact that we find ourselves working in the same hospital. Again.' She took a deep breath. 'It's unfortunate, I agree, but you had your chance to get rid of me. You could have let me get fired.'

'I didn't do it to protect your job and keep you here, if that's what you're thinking.'

No. That idea had been farfetched enough for Layla to have dismissed it at the time.

Almost.

'So why *did* you do it?' she asked quietly.

'Because I'm not going to let my past dictate my future. The Kirkpatrick case did enough damage already. I stood up for you because...because it was the right thing to do.'

Thanking him had seemed like the right thing to do, too, but he wouldn't let her. Now Layla wasn't even sure she wanted to thank him. Had he just been facing his own demons? Making them a part of a past that didn't matter any more?

She had to look away. 'Well...we're going to have to work together. I'm not about to leave a job I've only just started.'

'Neither am I.'

He was still angry. Layla could feel the waves of it reaching her across the distance she'd been careful to maintain between them. She could also feel other currents mixed in with the anger. Like his determination to succeed and the fierce intelligence with which he was assessing his options. And beneath all of that she could feel his raw magnetism and power. The charisma that Alex Rodriguez wore like a second skin.

There seemed to be nothing left to say.

They were at an impasse. Both of them struggling to take control of their present by focussing on the future and dismissing the past.

Could it be that easy?

Layla had to make an effort to swallow. 'Fine. Then let's start as we mean to go on from now on. I've set the agenda for the meeting. I'll look forward to hearing your presentation, Dr Rodriguez.'

Alex said nothing. With no more than another searing glance, he turned and left her office.

* * *

Two days later and people were filing into the small lecture theatre tucked away on an upper floor, along with
the operating theatres. Some were carrying Styrofoam
cups of coffee and paper bags containing sandwiches
and some were reading messages on their pagers. All of
them would have a notebook and pen available.

Fellow Texan, neonatal doctor Tyler Donaldson came
in, protectively ushering his now very pregnant fiancée, Eleanor, into a front-row seat where she would have
plenty of room. Eleanor smiled at Layla.

'Don't mind me if I have to sneak out to the bathroom,' she said. 'My bladder capacity is shrinking by
the day.'

'Yeah...' Tyler beamed proudly. 'And that little rodeo
rider in there likes to work out and use it for a punch-
ing bag.'

Layla returned the smile but said nothing. She wasn't
in the mood for baby talk and Tyler might be an old
friend but it wasn't exactly professional to sit there holding hands with Eleanor, was it?

There was a quiet buzz of conversation going on
and seats were being filled but there was still no sign
of Alex. Layla gave Ryan a questioning look, her head
tilted towards the door. As Alex's second-in-command,
surely he would know where the senior neurosurgeon
was? But Ryan merely shrugged and then turned to
his companion, a smile on his face as he responded to
some comment. The atmosphere in here was relaxed
and why wouldn't it be?

There was no blame, no shame for unsuccessful
cases but the discussion could get robust. What could
have been done differently? What *would* be done differ-

ently next time? Hindsight was a wonderful thing when it could be used for a good purpose. You could never say they didn't learn from mistakes around these parts.

Could Layla say that about herself?

Professionally, of course she could.

Personally? Layla suddenly became aware that she was tapping her foot impatiently. How long had she been doing that? Had anyone noticed? Her foot stilled.

Of course she could say that she learned from personal mistakes.

She hadn't got married again, had she?

She had challenged Alex, though. She hadn't heard a peep out of him since that tense exchange in her office and she'd been left wondering if he would back down and appear to present his case. Surely he would guess that a non-appearance would start people talking even more than if he'd shown up as her star turn of the day?

There was an air of expectancy in the room now. These were busy people. They only had an hour to spare and they were all giving up their lunch-breaks to attend. There were a few empty seats but that was normal. Some people couldn't make it on the day, even if they were rostered to present a case, but that was OK, too, because they always had more cases lined up than they ended up having time to discuss.

She'd give Alex exactly one more minute to show up.

'Aren't you supposed to be at Monthly Report?'

'Yep.' Alex Rodriguez was facing his half-brother, Cade. Both men were semi-crouched and already sweating in the midday September sunshine that bathed the small area out the back of the ambulance bay where a basketball hoop was attached to the wall.

Alex had control of the ball right now, bouncing it in sharp movements as his body wove from side to side, looking for an opening to get closer to the hoop.

'So why aren't you?'

'Could ask you the same question.'

'Hey, I was only going to listen. Aren't you supposed to be presenting a case?'

Alex ignored the question. With a lunge, he dived sideways, scooping up the ball and firing it at the hoop. With a resounding thump it hit the backboard and went through the net.

'*Yes*…'

Both men went for the ball as it bounced on the tarmac. This time Cade made contact first and gleefully took control.

'You may as well give up, bro. Go and have a shower and make Layla happy.'

'What the hell is that supposed to mean?'

'*Whoa*…' Cade caught the ball instead of bouncing it and spun it on his hand. 'Who put the burr under your saddle?'

Using Layla's Texan drawl, along with a phrase they'd both heard her use, was like rubbing salt into the wound. With a move Cade didn't see coming Alex knocked the ball from his hand and took off across the court, scoring another goal.

Cade laughed. Game on. For several minutes they played hard, ignoring the heat and the sweat and how out of breath they were getting.

No way was Alex going to go to that meeting and *make Layla happy*. It wasn't so much that this was obviously a public pat on the back for a case that had gone so well, it was the string-pulling that he could sense going on behind it.

OK, he'd done Layla a favour but he'd done it in order to face his own demons, not to protect her. He didn't want her thanks.

Hell, no...

Because if she got close enough to thank him properly, he knew exactly what could happen. Had already happened. That chemistry between them would explode and they'd end up in a clinch, kissing like there was no tomorrow.

And, God help him, he was not going to let it happen again.

Who the hell did Layla think she was that she could pull a string or two and have people dancing to her tune?

He'd told her that he didn't want to present. She'd had plenty of time to back down and change the agenda and she hadn't done so despite knowing that it could kick off a fresh wave of gossip. Well...he wasn't even going to put in an apology for the meeting.

He just wasn't going to show up. They might have to work together again but was going to do it on his terms, thank you very much.

She could deal with that. By herself.

This was getting borderline embarrassing.

From her position on the podium Layla nodded at the group. It was time to begin. Her heels sounded loud on the podium, rapping smartly on the wood as she moved to the microphone attached to the lectern. She tapped it gently to check it was on.

'Howdy, folks. Glad y'all could make it.' Her smile was bright. Along with good manners, Layla Woods had grown up knowing exactly how to present the perfect public face, no matter what was going on inside her head.

Or her heart, for that matter.

'Looks like our first presenter is missing in action,' she continued, 'so let's get the ball rolling with our second case. Dr Donaldson is going to share one of our neonatal department's case histories.'

'Thanks, darlin'…' Tyler reluctantly let go of Eleanor's hand and strolled up to the podium. He winked at Layla as he inserted a memory stick into the data projector.

Layla kept her smile in place with difficulty. She knew what that wink was about just as clearly as she could sense the significant looks being passed between the people seated in the tiered rows in here. They all knew that Alex's name was on the top of the agenda. Now they were all wondering if he really had an emergency keeping him away or if there was something else going on. Were some of those rumours circulating about a romantic involvement between Alex and Layla true?

'Meet Madeline,' Tyler Donaldson announced, as a photograph of a tiny, premature baby almost hidden by wires and tubes came up on the screen. 'Born at a gestation of twenty-five weeks, this li'l gal weighed in at six hundred and eighty grams and measured thirty-two centimetres. She was intubated immediately after birth and given positive pressure ventilation due to her prematurity.'

To outward appearances, Layla was listening attentively to the presentation of all the complications this baby had had but in reality she was trying to unravel the knot of anger forming in her gut.

He could have put in an apology for the meeting. Or arranged for Ryan to present the case. They could have both kept their dignity intact and made a fresh start by putting their professional lives onto some kind of an even keel. The gossip would be fuelled by his non-appearance with no explanation. Layla didn't like being the subject of gossip. She didn't like the ashes of the past being raked over. Would she ever get away from the mistake she'd made in getting involved with Alex in the first place?

Don't you mean get over *him*?

That tiny voice in the back of her mind got ruthlessly silenced. Layla glared at Tyler.

This was all his fault, wasn't it? They'd known each other practically their whole lives. Ty knew how badly her marriage had ended and how strained her relationship with her family was. OK, maybe he hadn't known about the affair that had spelt the end of that marriage, or that Alex had been the man she'd had an affair with, but it had been Ty who'd persuaded her to apply for the job here at Angel's.

The job that meant she and Alex were working at the same hospital.

Again.

Layla took a deep breath and tried to tune in to what Tyler was saying about the complex surgery baby Madeline had had to go through. The fleeting thought that his specialty had to be harder now that his fiancée was pregnant with his own baby only led Layla straight back to her own personal issues.

Like how she was going to deal with the tension between Alex and herself. It wasn't just about avoiding damage to their reputations, was it? There was still something there. Something powerful. That kiss had been more than enough to make it obvious. And, despite what Alex had said, she didn't believe that doing the right thing had been the only motive for defending her against the management board.

Did he care about her on some level?

Did she care about him?

Not like that. Layla may have fallen in love with him the first time around but the disaster the affair had created in her life had been enough for those emotions to morph into simmering resentment at how thoroughly her life had been derailed. Whatever was still hanging around was about lust, not love. But, man, that sexual chemistry hadn't lost any of its power, had it?

She just needed to learn to control it.

Like she tried to control everything else in her life?

Good grief, that little voice was annoying. A control freak? Her? Well…Layla had to admit she'd engineered what had been supposed to have happened today but look how well that had worked.

She was already planning how to get around it, though, wasn't she? To take control some other way. Instead of thanking him now, part of her wanted to let Alex know just how aggravated she was with the way he had dropped her into covering for his absence and fielding the ensuing curiosity.

She wanted to demonstrate that she was able to stand up for herself.

Like she had when he'd put her aside just before little Jamie's operation?

When she hadn't been prepared to stand aside quietly and she'd taken control and told him it was all over?

Why had she chosen the night before the surgery to

take her stand? She could have contributed to why Jamie's case hadn't turned out to be the kind of miracle that the case she'd asked Alex to present today was.

The guilt was still there, wasn't it? Not just that she'd been cheating on her husband but that she might have made a difference to Alex's performance that day.

And maybe *that* was why it had seemed so important that she got the chance to thank Alex.

And why he didn't want to hear it.

Why did it matter so much, anyway? It had been years and years ago. They'd both moved on.

Or had they?

Impossible not to remember that kiss…

It had been the last thing she had expected.

No. Maybe the *last* thing she had expected had been the way she'd responded to it. To have stepped so far back in time to when her desire for this man had made her throw her caution to the winds, along with too many of the values she'd grown up believing she held. They'd been fried in the heat that one touch from Alex could generate. Even now, Layla could feel a flicker of that heat, deep in her belly.

Was she blushing? Was that why there was this sudden silence all around her and why everybody seemed to be looking at her?

No. On an inward groan Layla realised that Tyler had finished his presentation. They were waiting for her, as the meeting's chairperson, to move things along.

Her smile was bright. 'Sorry, folks… Such an interesting case, I got lost in my thoughts. Anyone want to ask a question or add something?'

Several hands were raised and heart surgeon Molly Shriver got the nod.

'Can you talk us through your choice of antibiotic to deal with the pneumonia? And did you consider a blood transfusion immediately after the first surgery?'

Layla couldn't help looking past Molly, up into the dimmer corners of the lecture theatre where someone could have arrived unnoticed during Tyler's presentation by using the back stairs.

Not that she really needed the visual confirmation that Alex wasn't present. She could feel it. Like a shadow blocking the sun.

Forced to stop the hard physical activity due to exhaustion, Alex bent over, palms on his thighs, fighting to catch his breath again. Cade mirrored his action.

'It's working,' Cade panted. 'Think I've pulled the burr out from *my* saddle, anyway. How 'bout you?'

Again, Alex ignored the query. 'So what was your beef?'

'I'm fed up,' Cade growled. 'I was in charge of my department back in L.A. I don't like being told what to do like I'm just an intern. Getting squeezed out of the best cases. Having my decisions second-guessed.'

'You knew you were going to be second-in-charge when you took this job.'

'Yeah…I just didn't know how much I wouldn't like it. I'm beginning to think I should have followed your example and tried the other side of the world to escape. Australia is looking pretty damned attractive right now.'

'You didn't have something big enough to get away from.'

'Wanna bet?' Cade had caught his breath. He was moving again. His expression suggested he needed to blow off a bit more steam. He certainly didn't want to expand on that cryptic comment.

Alex tucked it away. He'd find out. He knew better than to push his half-brother to reveal more than he was ready to. It was too fragile, this newly re-formed relationship they'd managed to forge in the wake of the recent trouble.

Cade scored another goal. He was well ahead of Alex now.

'Anyway...' he panted, letting Alex get the ball again. 'It's all sorted, isn't it? The whole deal with that malpractice suit. You know I'm sorry for letting the cat out of the bag but we're good now, aren't we?'

'Yeah...' Alex was standing still, taking aim at the basket. Better than he could have hoped they'd ever be, that was for sure, given their history.

'And it's all out in the open and they're not going to fire you. Any more than they're going to fire Layla after you stood up for her.'

Alex missed the hoop and swore softly. He grabbed the ball as it bounced and took aim again.

He just couldn't get away from it, could he?

Away from Layla.

Away from the memories.

The demons he'd tried to deal with by running away after the malpractice suit that had followed the Jamie Kirkpatrick case were only part of the story.

Cade was trying to distract him from shooting the goal. Standing in front of him and waving his arms. He was grinning. He didn't know that Layla was another demon.

He'd heard she was divorced now. Well...no surprises there. Alex could feel sorry for the mug she'd conned into marrying her in the first place. Had she just dumped him—the way she'd dumped *him* when she'd got bored with their affair?

*Affair.*

Nasty little word but there was no getting away from the facts. He'd had an affair with a married woman. He wasn't proud of it and he certainly didn't want people to start talking about it. Had Cade been getting away from something that bad?

Now wasn't the time to find out. It was too hot for this and they both needed to go and shower and cool off.

Alex took another shot at the basket and the ball went through without even touching the backboard.

'Nobody's getting fired,' he finally agreed. 'And the whole mess taught me something very valuable.'

'Oh?' By tacit agreement, both men were calling it a draw and finishing the match. They high-fived each other and started walking back into the hospital.

'You don't beat demons by running away from them,' Alex told his younger brother. 'You can only beat them by confronting them.'

The sound Cade made was dismissive and Alex couldn't blame him for his disbelief.

He wasn't exactly confronting the demons that Layla represented, was he? He'd been avoiding her like the plague ever since she'd tried to thank him for standing up for her and saving her job. And then he'd marched into her office and told her to stay away from him. How was that supposed to sort anything out? And had he been entirely truthful? He'd told her that he'd gone to that board meeting to defend her because the Kirk-patrick case had done enough damage and it should be left in the past, but weren't the feelings Layla stirred part and parcel of the whole Jamie Kirkpatrick business anyway?

It had been so hard to put her aside so he could focus on that little boy's surgery. And he still suspected, deep in his heart, that the body blow of getting dumped the night before that high-profile operation had been why he hadn't been completely on top of his game that day. Yes, the demons were so intertwined they were impossible to separate.

Which meant he hadn't really confronted anything, despite letting the whole thing get aired in public again. Maybe he'd made it worse by giving Layla a reason to be grateful to him. He certainly hadn't helped his cause by giving her something to be angry about today.

Deliberately avoiding her hadn't done the trick. Fronting up and warning her hadn't achieved much either. And Layla was right about one thing. If they both wanted to keep their jobs here, they had to find a way of being able to work in the same hospital.

A corner of Alex's mouth lifted in a wry smile. Maybe he'd subconsciously realised that what he needed was to have Layla avoid him. The way she had after Jamie's death when she wouldn't even acknowledge him. All that was needed was a good push to get her started and what better way than a public refusal to let her jerk his strings?

Alex stood under the cool shower, letting the sweat sluice away. Be nice if the demons could get washed away as easily but he'd soon find out if he'd made life any easier for himself by what he'd just done. Monthly Report would be well and truly over by the time he was dressed again.

* * *

The discussion about Tyler's case was taking off now. They might finish a few minutes early but there certainly wouldn't be time for another case.

The gap left by the unpresented case would probably be old news by the time everybody headed back to their normal routines. They would all move on with ease.

The way Layla and Alex needed to if they were both going to keep their jobs and work together.

Maybe what was stopping them was that it was unfinished business.

And if there was something that bothered Layla more than being the subject of gossip it was having unfinished business hanging over her.

Mulling it over as she headed back to her office, Layla realised that dealing with this particular business would be dangerous. The tingle that kissed her skin as if she could still feel Alex's presence in this private room was enough of a warning. The way the memory of that kiss was lingering rang an even louder alarm.

But facing something dangerous…and winning… was kind of an attractive challenge.

And Dr Layla Woods had always found a challenge irresistible.

Besides, it could be good for both of them. She had a responsibility to try and ensure that the senior staff members could work together on good terms, didn't she?

Of course she did.

Layla took a moment to enjoy the view from her window. Plan B was beginning to shape up rather nicely.

# CHAPTER TWO

Everybody was waiting.

Expecting Alex Rodriguez to be taken to task by the chief of paediatrics for failing to put in an appearance or even the courtesy of an apology for the monthly report meeting.

Alex had caught more than one oddly expectant glance from people over the course of the afternoon following that meeting. When his path crossed again with that of Layla for the first time he was in the cafeteria for lunch the next day, and the air of anticipation around him was palpable. A public arena and an attentive audience to witness a senior staff member being told off was gold for feeding a grapevine.

Alex gritted his teeth and waited for the kind of acerbic comment that would let him know by how far he'd missed the mark in his professional responsibilities.

Instead, he was treated, along with everybody else snatching a quick meal, to one of those thousand-watt smiles that Layla was so good at.

'Good to see you're finding time to eat,' she said, with that husky Southern edge to her voice that always made her sound vaguely amused about something. 'I hear you're busier than a one-armed paper-hanger over there in Neurology.'

He waited for the kicker. The jibe about being so busy that he couldn't have found the good manners to let her know he couldn't make the meeting. But that smile didn't dim. With a flick of those tousled, shoulder-length blonde waves, Layla continued moving towards the food counter, leaving nothing but a faint scent of something deliciously fresh in her wake. Apples?

Realising that he was sitting there with his mouth half-open, trying to identify what flavour shampoo Layla used, was enough to make Alex aware of the unpleasant burn of embarrassment, but he needn't have worried. Everyone around him was still watching Layla. Especially the men. And the collective gaze was laced with admiration.

Definitely apples, he decided the next day when Layla brushed past him in the recovery room to visit with a small patient of hers who'd just undergone open heart surgery.

He knew it was a coincidence that had placed her patient right next to the little girl he'd just operated on to correct a spinal abnormality but did she have to stand on his side of the bed? Did she really have to be here at all?

'I've been so worried about this wee man,' he heard her say to the nurse. 'I just had to come and have a peek.'

'He's doing just fine,' the nurse reassured her. 'We'll be transferring him to PICU any time now.'

Recovery was an extension of the operating theatre suite. Alex's turf. As Chief of Paediatrics, Layla often got involved with the more serious cases that came into

Angel's and he'd often seen her in places like the paediatric intensive care unit. Even when she was stick-
ing to her own specialty of paediatric cardiology, she
would often have small patients who spent time in there
when their condition deteriorated or after they'd had
surgery. But he'd never come across her in the actual
recovery area and it felt like more than a professional
coincidence.

Was he getting paranoid or was Layla trying to get
in his face at every possible opportunity and…and *enjoying* it?

'Don't tell me…' Alex didn't try and erase the sar-
donic lilt to his words as the nurse sped off to attend to
another patient arriving from Theatre. 'You're regret-
ting your choice not to become a surgeon.'

'Not at all.' Layla's glance flicked the whole length
of his body and Alex instantly felt at a disadvantage.

Underdressed, standing here in his loose-fitting
scrubs. He still had a theatre cap on his head and he'd
only broken the top strings on his mask so it was hanging around his neck like a bib. Layla was wearing a
smart, close-fitting pencil skirt and a crisply ironed
blouse under her spotless white coat. And she had her
trademark high heels on. Alex was wearing white, plastic gumboots.

'I adore cardiology,' Layla continued. 'I get to make
the diagnosis and I get to enjoy the follow-up and see
the way lives improve after surgery. I don't have to
do the messy, in-between bit of adjusting the internal
plumbing.' Her gaze seemed to intensify. 'My surgical
rotation back when I was an intern showed me that it
wasn't where I wanted to be.'

That rotation had been when they'd met. When Layla

had become little Jamie's champion and she'd persuaded him to take on the toddler's complex surgery.

When they'd been together as far, far more than professional colleagues. Was that what Layla was really referring to here? Maybe he didn't want to find out. He backed down.

'I've just never seen you hanging around Recovery before,' he muttered. 'That's all.'

She knew, dammit. She knew exactly how uncomfortable he was with her presence in what had previously been a sacrosanct area for him.

*We're colleagues.* Her raised eyebrows managed to convey even more to the message. *We work in the same hospital. We are mature, professional people who are passionate about our careers. Deal with it.*

Fine. Alex *would* deal with it. He tilted his head towards the tiny patient in the bed.

'What was the procedure?'

'Just an ASD closure. But it was a big one and little Josh here is a real cutie. One of triplets.'

Triplets? Good grief... Why was nothing about Layla...*ordinary*?

Even this unusual visit was vaguely disturbing.

Any other doctor would be looking at the monitors or reading the recovery notes. Or at least quizzing the nurse. But not Layla. She was leaning over the tiny, unconscious boy. Finding a patch of skin that wasn't covered by an electrode for monitoring or tape that was holding an intravenous line in place. Stroking that skin with such a gentle touch that Alex couldn't look away.

'Hear what that nurse told me, honey?' he heard her murmur. 'You're doing just fine. You keep it up now.

Your momma and daddy aren't far away and they can't wait to see you.'

Alex forced his attention back to the monitors attached to his own patient but he couldn't ignore the knot in his gut. It tightened when he glanced back in time to see Layla on the point of leaving. She had two fingertips against her pursed lips and, having turned her head to check that the nurse wasn't watching, she took that tiny kiss and transferred it to the forehead of the unconscious toddler.

A tiny moment in time. A very personal moment. If Layla hadn't turned in his direction again as she'd straightened, she would never have known that she had been observed. Alex was busted. He wasn't going to pretend he hadn't been staring so he held her gaze steadily and it was gratifying to see the flush of colour that painted Layla's cheeks.

But she didn't look away. Her chin came up and the spark in her eyes was one of defiance.

*So I get emotionally involved with my patients*, the spark said. *Deal with that, too. I happen to think it makes me a better doctor.*

'See you later, Alex.'

'Yeah…I'm sure you will.'

The high heels of Layla's shoes beat a sharp tattoo as she exited the recovery room and, despite himself, Alex knew he was watching her leave with the same kind of expression that every male in the cafeteria had had the day before.

You had to hand it to her. Layla Woods had very decided opinions and more courage than you could shake a stick at to defend them. And that feistiness, wrapped up in such an attractive package, was the kind of challenge any red-blooded man would get drawn to.

Look at him. He knew the deadly consequences of rising to that challenge and he was still finding it difficult not to get sucked in all over again.

Alex looked down at his small patient. He had done the best he could for her with the surgery to correct the spinal malformation and he was confident that it had been a success. This little girl would soon be able to sit up and walk and catch up with the developmental milestones she had missed. Her parents were going to be thrilled and he would take a great deal of pleasure in following up on her progress.

He cared about her. A lot. But he wasn't going to start cuddling and kissing his patients. He'd learned long ago how dangerous emotional entanglements could be. Probably even before his mother had died.

Alex hadn't needed the gut-wrenching confirmation of that lesson represented by the disastrous notion that Layla might have been different enough to deserve his trust. And he wasn't going to lay himself open to the kind of heartache that came with losing a small patient that you'd got too attached to. He knew how to keep just the right amount of distance to make sure he stayed at the top of his game.

He just had to apply the same wisdom to his professional relationship with Layla, never mind how many times he found himself close to her. Or how many personal things he happened to notice.

Personal things like the kind of shoes she wore or shampoo she used were superficial and easily ignored. The personal detail he discovered about Layla a few days later nearly did his head in.

* * *

Plan B seemed to be going slightly astray.

The idea had been to show Alex that the past was well and truly behind them. That they could enjoy a professional relationship and put any lingering attraction behind them as well. Tuck it away, along with the malpractice suit and the way both their lives had been derailed.

But it seemed to be taking on a life of its own now.

Alex didn't like it that she was invading his space. Layla could feel the 'Oh, God, not *again*' vibe whenever she just happened to be in the same place at the same time. Like the cafeteria or Recovery or the intensive care unit or one of the wards. She was getting so good at this she didn't need to check his electronic calendar to guess where he might be next. Often her instinct put her in the right place. Or maybe fate was helping because her path seemed to be crossing with that of Alex far more often as she fulfilled her own professional duties.

Well, Alex had only himself to blame. The effect of her subtle campaign was magnified considerably by how successful Alex had been in trying to avoid her in the run-up to that meeting he'd stupidly decided to miss. This could have all blown over by now. She would have given Alex his moment in the limelight, taken the opportunity to say thank you in a heartfelt manner and they could have agreed that this was a fresh start for both of them.

Bygones could have been bygones.

But no… Alex had taken a stand and presented a challenge and she knew perfectly well that he would have been expecting her to front up and tear a strip or two off him because everybody knew that she didn't

hang back from necessary confrontation. The perfect
opportunity had presented itself the very next day, in
fact, in the staff cafeteria, with the bonus of a built-in
audience.

What a stroke of brilliance it had been, doing the
complete opposite of what they had all been expecting. Her ultra-friendly smile and the way she had simply ignored the whole issue had thrown Alex off guard
completely. He was still suspicious of her motives and
she couldn't blame him for not liking what was happening. She was in control here.

The problem was that she was enjoying herself. A
bit too much perhaps. She was quite confident of how
aware of her Alex was. She could sense the way he
watched her, like that time in Recovery. She could feel
the intensity of that gaze like a touch on her skin.

No. The real problem was the flip side of that particular coin.

She was equally aware of him.

Just how unhelpful this awareness was became strik-
ingly obvious a few days later after Layla had been
called to the emergency department to consult on a 'blue
baby' case that had been rushed in by ambulance. The
mother had had almost no prenatal care so the baby's
cardiac abnormalities had not been picked up prior to
birth and, to complicate matters, the young mother had
gone into labour and had given birth at home. With the
baby safely intubated and stabilised and now under the
care of the neonatal surgeons, Layla was free to leave
the department to carry on with the rest of her duties
when she spotted Alex.

He was standing just outside one of the resuscitation
rooms where the more serious cases were assessed and

stabilised. Right next door to the one she had been in. That small thrill of excitement and the way her heart rate picked up was due purely to the stroke of luck crossing his path in such an unexpected place. Neither of them had much to do with the emergency department so what were the odds of them both being here at the same time? That this would annoy Alex no end might be a kind of a bonus.

Except that he didn't even seem to be aware of her standing so close by. His attention was focussed on the woman he was with. White-faced and sobbing, she looked barely more than a teenager. She had long, dark, wildly curly hair and she was talking fast and loudly. In Spanish.

Alex was looking stunned. As though he had no idea how to handle the situation.

Layla had never seen him look like this.

She'd seen him in charge of emergency situations in Theatre. Running a resuscitation scenario in the intensive care unit. Dealing with distraught parents. But never once had she seen him look as if he wasn't in complete control.

Looking...vulnerable?

Well...she had once. When things had gone so disastrously wrong at the end of Jamie Kirkpatrick's surgery. She'd had to stand back and watch helplessly then.

She didn't have to now.

Layla moved swiftly towards them. 'Can I help you?' she said to the young woman. *'Te puedo ayudar? Digame lo que pasa...'*

Her Spanish was fluent. The woman grabbed her arm in relief and sobbed out her story. Alex looked, if anything, even more stunned when Layla turned back to him.

'Ramona says you're treating her baby. Felix?'

His nod was terse. 'He's got a skull fracture. I was hoping to get to the bottom of the story but the language barrier's suddenly got a lot worse.'

Layla asked Ramona a question and then translated the response. 'His brother hit him with a toy brick.'

She could see the total disbelief in Alex's face. 'I'm talking about a fracture here. A *broken* skull. An *unconscious* child.' His voice was so tense it cracked.

Layla's brain sent out the kind of alert signal that any Chief of Paediatrics would be wise to pay attention to. It had been known to happen, hadn't it? She'd read of more than one case where parents had had children taken away from them by social services and had been prosecuted for child abuse.

One sprang to mind immediately, of an eight-month-old boy whose sibling had hit him with a toy aeroplane and caused a fracture. And what about the Tommy Jenner case a few months ago when the child-abuse screen had been started and then they'd found that Tommy had actually been injuring himself because of the seizures caused by his brain lesion?

Alex needed to be careful of what he was saying here but Layla found that she was thinking of something else entirely as she stared at him. Had she really not noticed before how those glimmers of grey had crept into his jet-black hair? The way those lines at the corners of his eyes had deepened over the years they hadn't seen each other? Had she really forgotten the way those chocolate-brown eyes could darken when something emotionally intense was going on, like anger or…physical passion?

Heavens...they looked positively black at the moment.

Ramona had picked up the tone of Alex's voice. Looking terrified, she made a huge effort to pull herself together and change languages.

'No...don't say those words. No person hurt my baby. I...I *love* him.'

The anguish in her eyes and broken words was heart-breaking. Alex put his hand on the young woman's shoulder.

'Try and calm down, Ramona. I won't ask any more questions now. We've got Felix stabilised and we'll be taking him up to surgery in a few minutes.'

'*Què*? I...no understand...'

Layla translated but she couldn't look away from where Alex's hand was still resting on Ramona's shoulder. She could feel that hand herself.

'Ask her if her husband's on the way,' Alex ordered.

But Ramona understood that.

'Not husband. Boy...friend. I was...' With an impatient head shake and hand movements she reverted to rapid Spanish and Layla had to relay the information.

'She was already pregnant with Felix when she met him. He's bringing in her older son. She's scared that you're going to call the police and she doesn't want to get into trouble.' It was quite possible there was an issue concerning illegal immigration here. Layla bit her lip, wondering if this was another alert signal her new position meant she should be worrying about.

The hand had dropped now. Layla watched as Alex's fingers curled into a fist but that was the only sign that something was disturbing him very deeply. That and the sense of raw power he was exuding. Right now that power was all about anger on behalf of a defenceless small child. Did he know for sure that his little patient's head injury had not been accidental? Layla wouldn't want to be standing in his way if he was planning to do something about such a conviction.

When he looked at Layla, she knew he was barely aware of her.

'Tell her that my only concern is treating her son.'

Alex left the impression of power in his wake and it stayed with Layla long after leaving Ramona with one of the nurses. She was left with a whole kaleidoscope of impressions whirling around her head, in fact.

The tension in Alex's face. The image of his hand on Ramona's shoulder. The way those dark, dark eyes had seemed to look right through her.

Memories… That first time they'd made love in the wake of her being so wound up after a blazing row with Luke. The urgency and the mind-blowing *heat* of that encounter. The unbelievable bliss in which it had culminated…

The feel of his lips against hers, which she'd experienced again not very long ago. The sheer wanting that it could conjure up every single time…

Oh, yes. It was just as well Alex was nowhere near where he might be able to see what was whizzing through her head because any control Layla felt she'd had in following this fool plan of hers had just gone out the window.

Concentrating on what she had to do for the rest of her day was quite a tall order. Layla was still feeling out of kilter by the time she got to the end of her list, long after most staff members had finished their days and gone home for dinner. She always liked to pop into all the intensive care units before she went home, to make sure she was in touch with how all Angel's most seriously unwell children were doing.

Her little 'blue' baby was in the cardiac unit, having had surgery to correct the abnormality she had been born with. All was well in NICU, the neonatal intensive care unit. PICU was her last stop. Maybe because she was a little nervous at crossing paths again with Alex today?

A little nervous? Judging by the way she actually jumped when she heard the sound of his voice even before she saw him, she was as jumpy as spit on a hot skillet.

'For God's sake…a skull fracture with acute subdural and epidural bleeding. You can't tell me a two-year-old kid can throw a wooden brick hard enough to cause that kind of an injury.'

'Are there any other potential signs of abuse?'

Another male voice. And they were both talking quietly, probably confident that their intense conversation was private. Had they left the unit for precisely that reason?

Layla stopped in her tracks, unsure of whether to round the corner where she'd have to walk past them to get to the locked door of the intensive care unit. The indecisiveness was an alien sensation and she didn't like it at all. She shifted her weight from one foot to the other, fingering her security badge, which would allow her access through that locked door.

'I don't know.' Alex's voice was a growl. 'I haven't had a chance to check him over properly yet. I've been too busy trying to save the poor little tyke's life. My sus-

picions are more than enough to base a report on and it
needs to be filed within thirty-six hours of admission.'

'You need to be careful. Do you remember the first
time I went to the monthly report meeting? Who was
that kid you presented the case on? The one who's been
on chemo for months and you're going to think about
operating on soon?'

'Tommy Jenner.' Alex sounded impatient now. He
didn't want to change the subject.

'You presented that case as a warning, didn't you?
Not to make assumptions that just might be wrong.
The *last* thing you need is another malpractice suit on
your hands.'

'Are you telling me to stand back and say nothing?
You, of all people, should know better than that, Cade.
We *both* know the kind of damage that can do, don't
we?'

'Yeah, yeah…point taken. But that's exactly why you
need to tread carefully, man. You're too wired to see the
worst-case scenario. You know too much.'

Layla was standing very still now, her eyes wide.
What on earth was all that supposed to mean?

'You're following protocol,' Cade continued. 'Treating the child is number one. You can order a child-abuse
screen and do the other tests you need, like X-rays to
look for old fractures. The kid's safe and you've got
some time up your sleeve. You need to cool down.'

Having Layla appear around the corner probably
wouldn't help Alex to cool down. She found herself
backing away. Turning, ready to leave, only to find herself face to face with a man who had a small boy with
him. The child was about two or three years old and he
was a reluctant companion. The man had a grip above

the boy's elbow and was half pulling, half shoving him along. With long, greasy-looking hair and the skin of his arms beneath his T-shirt barely visible between tattoos, the man looked distinctly menacing.

'Get a move on,' he snarled down at the child, ignoring Layla. 'We're going to find your mother and then I'm outta here. I'm done with babysitting someone else's snivelling brat.'

He swept past Layla and around the corner. He practically banged into Alex and Cade.

Layla was hot on the man's heels. She didn't need the strong whiff of alcohol that reached her nostrils to know that a very volatile situation was forming.

'Whoa...' It was Cade who held up a hand to ward off a collision. 'Take it easy.'

'I'm in a hurry,' the man responded. He ignored Alex and walked past Cade. 'What...is that door *locked*? What kind of a joint is this? I thought it was a hospital, not a bloody prison.'

Layla was watching Alex. She could see he had assessed what was going on with the speed and intelligence she had learned to expect from him long ago. He was also putting two and two together as fast as she had. A young man arriving at the intensive care unit with a small boy. His patient's mother was inside the unit with her son. The baby had an older brother who had, supposedly, caused his severe head injury.

Alex caught her gaze and she felt that tingle of connection. Of knowing they were on exactly the same wavelength.

But there was more to this than a surgeon worried about his patient or a doctor who found treating a case of child abuse appalling. The shadows she could see in

Alex's gaze created a flood of questions. She'd always been aware of that dark side to him, hadn't she? She'd never had the chance to find out how it had got there. She'd been happy to just let it add to the frisson of danger that had gone with getting close to this man. The excitement of the illicit affair.

And, right now, it was more than just wanting answers to those questions…she wanted to defuse this situation. Or was it more than that even? That squeezing sensation in her chest suggested that she wanted to… make it better somehow. For Alex.

As if he read something of that in her face, his gaze jerked away from her to the stranger.

'You're Ramona's boyfriend, aren't you?' Alex sounded calm. Dangerously so.

'Who wants to know?'

'I'm Alex Rodriguez. Felix's neurosurgeon. I'm the person who's been operating on Felix this afternoon. Getting some of the blood out of his skull before it did too much damage to his brain.'

'Good for you.' The man eyed Alex up and down. More up than down. Both Alex and his brother towered over this stranger by at least six or seven inches. Layla could see that he was practised in assessing another man's strength but if he was intimidated by his male company he didn't show it. He stepped closer to Alex. 'If you're a doctor, you can let me in through that door. I've got a right to see Ramona.'

Alex was taking a breath. Layla could see the way his eyes narrowed as he smelt the alcohol. 'I'd like a word with you first, if you don't mind.'

'I do mind.' Layla saw the way the man shoved the little boy to one side and then curled his fists.

The little boy staggered sideways and bumped into Cade, who caught him as he started sobbing. 'You're OK, buddy,' he said.

'Shut up, Cody, or you'll be sorry,' the man warned.

'Like Felix was?' Alex's query was almost conversational.

'Alex...' Cade's tone was a warning.

The men were squaring off at each other. Layla could feel the fury of Alex's stare even though it was fastened firmly on the man directly in front of him. The tension was indescribable. Any second now and all hell would break loose. Alex would flatten Ramona's low-life boyfriend and then what? She wouldn't be trying to thank him for saving *her* job. She'd be fighting a losing battle trying to save his.

Not going to happen.

Without pausing to think about what she was doing, Layla stepped in between the two men just as both men raised their fists.

The vicious shove she received from behind was meant to get her out of the way but, in fact, it slammed her against Alex's rigid body. He had no choice but to lower his fists to catch hold of her before she fell sideways. It still felt like she was falling but she was encased in an astonishingly powerful grip.

From the corner of her eye she saw the fist aimed at Alex, which would have connected with the side of her head if Alex hadn't hauled her out of harm's way.

He only held Layla long enough for her to feel that strength and all that leashed power. To feel the pounding of his heart against her own for no more than a second. And then he let go of her and moved so swiftly the attacker didn't have a chance.

'That's *enough*.' Alex grabbed the raised arm of the attacker and then twisted it behind the man's back.

'*Ow*...lemme go,' the man snarled. The words turned into a whimper of pain as Alex clearly tightened his grip.

Layla, Cade and little Cody were all staring, wide eyed.

'Call Security,' Alex told Cade. 'Layla, take Cody in to find his mother.'

Layla did as she was told. She held out her hand. 'Come on, honey. I'll just bet your momma is going to be so happy to see you.'

Behind her, she could hear Cade talking urgently to Alex. 'I'll sit on him till Security gets here. You need to go and cool down before you talk to them. I'll tell them you got paged.'

'No way...' The refusal was almost drowned by a stream of obscenities and threats from Ramona's boy-friend.

Layla used her swipe card to gain entry to the unit. As the doors closed behind Cody and herself she could only hope that Alex could control his fury. It didn't matter what the man was guilty of—a member of staff in an altercation with a parent figure would be a dismissible offence.

She found a staff member to take care of Cody and filled them in on what had happened. She even spoke briefly to Ramona and learned that Felix had come through his surgery with flying colours and everybody was very pleased with how he was doing. It was only a few minutes before she could head back to see what was happening on the other side of the door. With a curious mix of both relief and disappointment she found Alex was nowhere to be seen. Ramona's boyfriend was also gone from the scene and the security guard talking to Cade had finished whatever he needed to do.

'I'll go and have a word with the boy's mother,' he said. 'And I'll catch up with Dr Rodriguez when he's done with that emergency.'

Layla pinned Cade with a look that told him she wasn't leaving without some answers.

'Where's Alex?'

Cade shrugged. 'Gone. I thought he should cool off a bit before he started talking to the cops.'

There was a moment's silence as they stared at each other. Cade looked...defensive? As if he was challenging Layla to criticise Alex for coming on too strong. She weighed her words.

'I heard you guys talking,' she said carefully. 'What did you mean by Alex knowing too much?'

She could see the shutters come down. Cade shrugged again, a gesture that told her this was between brothers and none of her business. And then his eyebrow rose.

'Is it true what I've heard around here? That there's something going on between you and Alex?'

Was this a case of attack being the best form of defence? Or was it a brother looking after a brother? If Layla wanted an honest answer from Cade, maybe he deserved the truth first.

'Not now,' she told him. 'There's...history. We were together way back. At the time of the Kirkpatrick case. You'd know about that.'

A sharp nod from Cade. 'It's what made me get in touch with Alex after not seeing him for years. Not that

I got much of a chance to spend time with him before he took off to Brisbane.'

'It messed up a lot of things,' Layla agreed. 'But what's important right now is that I owe my job to Alex and I'm not going to let him get into trouble over what just happened here if I can help it.'

Cade's nod was relieved. 'Just as well. The creep's telling everybody that Alex started it. Just laid into him without any provocation.'

'I'll sort it,' Layla promised. But she wasn't letting Cade off the hook just yet. '*After* I've talked to Alex, that is. Now, are you going to tell me where he is so I can do that before the cops start looking for me?'

Cade sighed. 'He didn't say where he was going but I'd guess he's where he always is when he wants to burn off some steam. Where we both go.'

'Which is?'

'The hoop-shooting court out the back of the ambulance bay.'

# CHAPTER THREE

THE SLAP OF the ball against the palm of his hand was hard enough to be causing pain.

Firing the ball towards the hoop with such aggression before he'd warmed up properly had ripped a bit of muscle, too, so that every subsequent attempt at a goal sent a stabbing sensation through his shoulder. On top of that, Alex had been going hard enough to be out of breath enough to make his lungs burn and create a satisfyingly deep ache in his chest every time he tried to suck in some more oxygen.

But he wasn't ready to stop yet. No way.

This felt like a fight to the death.

OK, he'd been wrong about Tommy but he'd known in his gut that Felix had been the victim of abuse from the moment he'd seen him. He should have had the cops there waiting for that creep of a father figure to turn up.

He'd wanted to kill the guy. Or at least hurt him enough to make him stop and think about what he'd done to an innocent child. Felix was a *baby*, for God's sake. He had no chance to defend himself in any way. He'd still feel the pain, though, wouldn't he? And the shock of such a betrayal from a person he had to trust because his survival depended on it.

His breath coming in ragged gasps, Alex did another circuit of the court at high speed, hammering the ball on the tarmac with every step, getting back to the point where he could make another leap and fire the ball at the hoop as fast as he could.

He'd been luckier than Felix. Ten years old and big for his age before the abuse from his stepfather had really started. Big enough to be fiercely determined to protect his little brother. Strong enough to stand up to a man who'd made it very clear he didn't give a damn about his dead wife's kid.

He hated this part of his job. Hated the memories that came with cases like this. Felt consumed with anger that his time and skills had to be used to fight something that should never, ever have happened in the first place. In a perfect world he could devote his life to being the absolute best in dealing with the kind of things that weren't preventable. The kind of complicated lesions that came out of nowhere and threatened to blow a loving, *real* family apart.

Everybody knew he was well on the way to being the best. What they didn't know was that he was driven to it by the mix of guilt and determination that he had to live with for ever. Guilt over what had happened in the little Jamie Kirkpatrick case. Determination that it would never, ever happen again. That nothing, and nobody, would ever put him off his game.

And that was under threat.

It wasn't just the anger about child abuse in general that Alex was trying to burn off here. Or the fury and disgust at coming face to face with the perpetrator in a single case. Part of what was pushing him on and on despite the pain right now was fear. This threat was huge.

Because of the guilt that had spurred his determination in the first place.

Because the reason he hadn't been on top of his game for little Jamie was back in his life again.

And because the pull of it was unbearable.

It had been bad enough earlier today when he'd heard her speaking *Spanish*, for God's sake…

He could probably have conversed with Ramona himself except that he'd shut the door so successfully on the language he'd heard so much of in his earliest years. The Rodriguez family had kept close ties with their culture but his mother had refused to speak Spanish after his father had died. Phrases had slipped out in emotional times, though, on the occasions she'd got cross. More often when she'd been happy, like when she'd been giving him a cuddle and kiss to say goodnight.

It was a language that touched something very deep inside Alex. It had roots in a happy time that was so long ago it was only a fairy-tale. Hearing Layla speaking it so fluently had given him a chill down his spine. Made him realise that there was more connecting him to this woman that he'd thought.

Pulling him back.

But he hadn't realised the terrifying power of that pull until a few minutes ago. When he'd been so consumed with that anger towards Ramona's boyfriend that he might have ignored Cade's warning about what the consequences might be until…until Layla had stepped between them and everything had changed in a heartbeat.

The need to protect her had come with the same kind of automatic speed that he'd practised as a kid, making sure that Cade wasn't going to get in the way of his father's fists. And *that* had become more important than anything else.

And then that low-life had pushed her and she'd slammed up against his body and, as inconceivable as it should have been given the circumstances, the awareness of her warmth and softness and...just that she was *Layla* had messed with his head completely.

The desire to hurt the creep had been diluted by the relief that Layla was safe. The memories were jangled and confused. Cade had been right. He'd needed to get away to cool off and clear his head.

Was he succeeding?

It didn't feel like it. Another circuit of the court and the muscles in his legs were burning now. Every pore was releasing sweat in a vain attempt to cool him down and he felt light-headed for a moment because he wasn't getting enough oxygen.

But he still kept going. The anger may have worn off but he still had too many other emotions curdling his blood.

He had to fight the threat. Find a way through it. He wasn't going to let his life get derailed again. He'd learned his lessons.

Not instantly, of course. He'd gone from his disastrous fling with a married woman to falling into bed with Callie Richards, one of his new colleagues in Brisbane. The lust had burned off fast enough, though, and he'd been left with a friendship he knew they'd have for ever. Callie was just like him. Burned by love to the same extent and determined that it would never interfere with her life again.

She'd tell him to do whatever it took to forget and then move on.

Like they had, after their fling had fizzled out. They'd been able to salvage a true friendship and work together without this gut-wrenching tension he was trying to get past now.

It was so hard fighting the past here. Especially now. The memories of Jamie. And Tommy. And now Felix.

And not just the *memories* of Layla. He had to deal with the *reality* of her. Every day. Every minute of the day it had started to feel like. That kiss. The feel of her body against his so recently upstairs. That disturbing, automatic need to protect her.

He had to deal with it. Or he'd have all his demons snapping at his heels for the rest of his life and he'd never find peace.

Alex was finally forced to stop moving and catch his breath.

Exhausted now, he could start to push everything out of his head. Except for the knowledge that he had to find a way through this and that he had no idea where to start.

Give him a case that was complicated enough to scare anyone else off and he was fine. He could make a plan. Step by step. A thorough investigation and then treatment with the goal of a cure lighting the path.

Work was great like that. But personal stuff?

Callie might know what he needed to do. She was a touchstone for advice.

Maybe Cade could help. He'd lived with the same background of violence and he'd only been protected until Alex had abandoned him and walked out when he'd been sixteen. Cade had been justifiably angry but they were sorting out that emotional minefield now. They were brothers again and that was thanks to Cade making the first move so maybe he would have a clue where you got started on a journey to make peace with the past and move on.

He certainly needed to talk to someone. If he didn't find an outlet for the emotions he couldn't suppress, he'd go crazy.

Things weren't hurting quite so much now. A few more minutes of this over-the-top physical activity and he could go and have a shower. With a bit of luck he'd be too tired to even think after that.

Layla had gone through the emergency department and out the automatic doors that led to the ambulance bay. There was a crew unloading a young patient who appeared to be having a severe asthma attack. He was sitting bolt upright on the stretcher, clutching a nebuliser mask to his face. His anxious parents gave Layla a hopeful look as if the stethoscope around her neck and perhaps the seniority her white coat advertised meant she would pause on her way and put things right, but all she could offer was a sympathetic smile.

She'd never been around the back of the ambulance bay before. As far as she knew, this was where all the rubbish skips were lined up ready for collection so there'd never been a reason to go there. Tucked into the corner, however, and brightly lit by the powerful security lights, was a good-sized patch of tarmac. The backboard and hoop were securely attached to one of Angel's walls.

Alex had clearly been working out without a pause since she'd last seen him. He was wearing nothing more than some shorts, a singlet and trainers, and his exposed skin gleamed with sweat.

And, oh, man…there was a lot of exposed skin.

Standing at the end of the line of rubbish skips and not directly under a light, Layla knew she was probably invisible. Alex was so focussed on his lonely game that he probably wouldn't have noticed her anyway, even if she was out in the open. She should call out or something because it felt suddenly as if she was seeing something private but when she opened her mouth Layla found it was inexplicably dry and no sound emerged.

Even if the overhead lights weren't picking Alex out from the surrounding darkness like spotlights, it would have been impossible to look away. This was the image of a very well-built, very fit man. There wasn't an ounce of fat on Alex Rodriguez. Muscles rippled and tendons appeared like ropes on his thighs and arms as he ran and twisted, changing direction and gathering speed before firing a shot at the goal. Layla found herself holding her breath every time, waiting for the crack of the ball against the backboard and the satisfying slide of it going through the net.

There wasn't a woman alive who wouldn't be impressed by Alex's body even when he was fully clothed and standing absolutely still. To watch him display this level of fitness and physical acuity was mesmerising. Erotic, in fact. She could hear the rasp of Alex's ragged breathing and the occasional grunt of effort. She could almost feel the body heat coming at her in waves and smell the salty tang of his sweat.

Her mouth might be dry but there was another part of Layla that most certainly wasn't. Her breathing rate had picked up as well and her knees were actually feeling weak, like those of some swooning heroine from a story like *Gone With The Wind* or something.

When Alex finally stopped to catch his breath, Layla ordered herself to get a grip and focus on what she'd come here for.

Which was what, exactly?

To talk about what had just happened outside the intensive care unit, of course. So that they could make sure they were singing from the same hymn book and that, if necessary, she could use her position to make sure Alex didn't get into any trouble over this.

And…if that went well enough, maybe she'd push him just a little bit and try and find out what Cade had meant about Alex knowing too much. What it was that had made him shut her out so convincingly.

Layla didn't like being shut out.

She pulled herself together enough to think she could manage to start this conversation but by then Alex had started running again. Not nearly as fast and furiously as he had been when she'd arrived. The anger he'd been burning off must be spent and that was a good thing. He probably wouldn't mind being interrupted now. Swallowing hard, Layla walked away from the rubbish skip and out into the open where he couldn't fail to see her when he started a new circuit after the next goal.

It wasn't so good that she'd have to talk to him while he was more than half-naked and dripping with sweat, given the ache of raw desire she could still feel pulsing in her belly, but Layla already had a plan in place. She'd tell him to have a quick shower and then they'd grab a coffee. She'd wait outside the door of wherever he was going to have a shower to make sure that she got to talk to him first.

The clock was ticking. The police were probably paging him already.

\* \* \*

Alex became aware of Layla's presence the moment she stepped into the periphery of his visual field but he totally ignored her while he did another circuit of the court.

He could guess why she'd come looking for him. Well…she could stand there for another minute or two. The fact that the few items of clothing he was wearing were now dripping wet and clinging to his body didn't bother him at all. The physical activity and his success in burning off that anger made him feel powerful. In control. Layla, standing there with her pretty skirt and her hair getting ruffled by the warm evening breeze, looked feminine and fragile. Definitely on the back foot.

The final goal was accompanied by a snort of something close to laughter from Alex.

Layla *fragile*? Not in this lifetime.

With a final bounce Alex caught the ball. He turned and walked decisively to where Layla was standing. He couldn't miss the way her eyes widened as he got closer. Or the way her breath hitched, allowing just a tantalising glimpse of cleavage to peep over the scooped neckline of her blouse. She even averted her gaze when he got within touching distance.

Oh, yeah…Layla wasn't very comfortable right now.

'We need to talk,' she said.

Alex let one corner of his mouth curl upwards. 'Sure. Unless you'd prefer me to shower first?'

'That…would probably be a good idea. I…um… wouldn't want you to catch a chill or something.'

'I'll only be a minute.' Alex tilted his head towards the rarely used facility built into one corner of the am-

bulance bay. 'We often use the shower in the decontamination room over there.'

'Fine. I'll wait out here.'

The decontamination room was big enough to allow
a stretcher to get wheeled in. It was designed to deal
with a situation like people or equipment being in contact with a toxic chemical or potential infection. Completely tiled, there were overhead showers as well as
hand-held sprays over a tilted floor with large drains.
There were also big tubs and shelves that held stacks
of clean towels and other items that might be needed,
like gowns, gloves and masks.

Alex stripped off and got under the shower, pumping
some soap from the container attached to the wall. He
scrubbed some lather through his hair and then sluiced
it off, letting the water rain on his face and onto his
chest. He shook his head when he turned the water off
but still had rivulets running over his skin as he stepped
off the tilted floor to reach for a towel.

He felt the cool touch of the breeze on his back and
knew the door had opened behind him. With a corner
of the towel dangling from one hand, he turned to see
Layla closing and locking the door behind her.

'What the *hell* do you think you're doing?'

She was leaning against the door now, facing him
but with her eyes closed.

'There's a cop out there. The squad car's parked in
the last ambulance slot. I didn't want them to see me
yet. Or find you yet. I…couldn't think what else to do.'
Layla opened her eyes. 'Sorry.'

Alex was trying to process this. She was hiding from
the police? Because she had some misguided notion that
she could protect *him*? Why did she want to do that?

In the time it took for the thoughts to take their turn Alex was also processing the way Layla's gaze dropped. Slowly. Travelling down his body and then up again. The way her pupils dilated. The way the very tip of her tongue appeared to moisten her lips.

Oh...God... What was it about the chemistry between them? This was way more intense than the atmosphere had been before that kiss. Alex could feel the oxygen being sucked out of the air around them. That final plunge before the electricity exploded. If he didn't do something...anything...right *now*, they would both be consumed by the flames and there would be no turning back.

But it was too hard to even think, let alone move.

He was as naked as a jaybird. With his hair all spiky and drops of water caught on the damp whorls of hair on his chest. Hair that arrowed down to where his fist was holding the edge of the towel.

She knew what was barely concealed by that drape of towelling. She knew what that hand was capable of doing when it wasn't busy holding something. Maybe if every cell in her body wasn't screaming for more than the memory of that touch she could have handled this. But then Layla's gaze dragged itself upwards until it snagged with Alex's mouth and she knew she was completely lost.

She couldn't look away. The only thing her brain was capable of was willing those lips to come closer. To touch her own.

A pager sounded. Hers? Maybe Alex's, coming from the pile of his clothing that was on the bench. They were both off duty so it was most likely to be something connected to the incident upstairs. Something that should have been enough to break the unbearable sexual tension in this small, clinical space.

It certainly broke the impasse but not in the way Layla had expected. With a muttered curse Alex moved.

Not to look for his pager.

Towards Layla.

His fingers caught in her hair as they curled around her neck. She closed her eyes, instinctively tipping her head back. Exposing her neck to him. Parting her lips. Waiting for *that* moment...The touch of his lips...his hands...his tongue. The moment when nothing else in the world mattered.

And when it came, it was better than she could have imagined. That unexpected kiss, weeks ago now, had erased the first shock of their bodies meeting again. This time it was all about what they knew they could give each other. What they craved like an addict denied his fix for too long.

How was it that the passion could be so white hot and desperately urgent and yet it could feel gentle at the same time? That buttons could come undone and not ping onto the tiles like bullets?

The sounds echoed around them. The fast breathing. The groans of pleasure so intense it was painful. Did the sound come from her own throat when Alex's hand cupped her breast, his thumb pulling the lace of her bra aside so that his lips could find her nipple?

Of course it did. But it was matched by the low growl that came from Alex. Her cry was much louder moments later when her skirt was hitched up and she was touched where she wanted it most.

It wasn't enough. Layla could feel the hard tiles

against her back. She had the hardness of Alex's body against her breasts and her belly. Her own hands sought the hardness she knew she would find. That she couldn't live without for another heartbeat.

This was wild. Irresponsible and totally, absolutely irresistible.

Layla felt her panties being dragged down.

*Yes...*

She felt herself being lifted. She wrapped her arms around Alex's neck and her legs around his hips. It would only be a matter of seconds before she got tipped off the world into paradise and maybe the bliss wouldn't last nearly long enough but...oh, *God*...nothing was this good and never could be.


For a long, long minute there was nothing but the sound of them both trying to catch their breath.

Not a word was spoken as they finally peeled apart. Layla fixed her clothing while Alex got dressed.

He checked his pager.

'Cade's looking for me.' Alex had to clear his throat. 'He's talking to the cops.'

'We still need to talk.' Heavens, her voice had come out all husky too, from the aftermath of passion.

'We'll do it on the way. Come with me?'

A bubble of wild laughter threatened to escape from Layla. *I just did*, she thought. And then the realisation hit her. Of what had just happened. How huge it was—to her, at any rate. Of how weird it was not to be saying anything about it. Of how enormous the new problem had just been created. What did it mean and, more importantly, what on earth were they going to do about this?

Maybe it was too big to know what to say yet. Layla stared at Alex and he held her gaze. She could see the kind of peace that only came from ultimate physical satisfaction. But she could also see confusion there. Regret, maybe? She didn't want to hear him say anything to confirm that.

'And, yeah...I reckon we do need to talk.' Alex still hadn't broken eye contact. 'We'll do that real soon.'

With a nod Layla followed him to where they needed to be now.

The promise was enough. Alex was a man of his word. They *would* talk soon and somehow, between them, they would be able to sort everything.

The tension between them had been resoundingly broken, that was for sure. Plan B had succeeded in a most unexpected way. Now all they needed was a new plan. One that would enable them to find a way forward.

A plan that Layla couldn't begin to formulate because it was going to be very different. And it required input from both of them.

# CHAPTER FOUR

'YOU DIDN'T...' A gasp was followed by an echo of incredulous feminine laughter over the international phone line. 'Oh, my God, Alex. You *idiot*.'

'Hey...I rang you for some advice, Callie Richards. Not a character assassination.'

'OK. Sorry, mate. But...but *Layla*? Wasn't she the final straw that drove you over to this side of the world?'

'Yeah...I *know*...' Alex scrubbed his fingers through his hair as he stood, clad only in his boxer shorts, beside the open windows of his Manhattan apartment, trying to catch a hint of breeze in the middle of this sultry Indian-summer night. He sighed heavily. 'I *am* an idiot. I thought I could handle it, you know? Stay the hell away from her, even though we're working in the same place. But there she was...'

'You were at *work*. Even *we* never did anything that crazy.'

Being ashamed of himself was a very alien sensation for Alex. He tried to ignore the unpleasant squirm in his gut.

'I hope some of your brain cells were still active and that you used a...'

Alex had to cut her off. Callie may be an ex-lover

and his best friend but there were limits to how candid
he wanted this conversation to be. 'No,' he snapped.
'They're not something I generally have on hand when
I'm at work.'

There was a moment's shocked silence on the line.
She didn't need to tell him how stupid he'd been. How
irresponsible. That he was thirty-eight years old, not
eighteen, and he should have known better.

'It just happened, Cal. I can't undo the past, no matter how recent. What I'm trying to figure out here is
what the hell am I going to do about it *now*?'

Callie's voice had a sharper edge. 'What did Layla
have to say about it?'

'That we need to talk.' Alex wasn't about to admit
it, even to the woman he considered to be the closest
friend he'd ever had in his life, but the prospect was terrifying. He didn't want to have that conversation with
Layla. Didn't want to be that close to her again until
he was absolutely confident he could handle it. And
his level of confidence in that situation had been badly
shaken. Destroyed?

'She's right,' Callie told him.

'I *am* talking,' Alex growled. 'To *you*.'

Callie's voice softened. 'And it's great to hear you,
mate. I miss having you around.'

There was another short silence that seemed to con-
tain a sigh of regret. Of them being a world away from
each other? Sadness that their brief fling when Alex had
first gone to Brisbane had burned itself out so convincingly that nothing more than the chance of friendship
was left in its wake? Not that the friendship wasn't wonderful. They were so alike they could have easily come

from the same genetic pool. Callie was a soul mate in the way a sister could have been.

'You've hardly called since you moved to the Big Apple,' Callie added. 'Not good enough.'

'I know. I'm sorry. It's been hectic.'

'Yeah, yeah...I know what you're like, Alex. But being a workaholic to escape personal stuff might not be the whole answer.'

It was Alex's turn to let a snort of laughter escape. 'That's the pot calling the kettle black.'

'So? I'm an expert.' Callie was unrepentant. 'I know what I'm talking about and I'm better at it than you.'

'OK. If you're such an expert, tell me what I'm supposed to do about this. I don't want to get tangled up with Layla Woods again. With anyone, for that matter.'

'That might have been your first mistake,' Callie said seriously. 'If you hadn't taken that vow of celibacy after our...after we...' She cleared her throat. 'Anyway...you're not cut out to be a monk, Alex Rodriguez. If you'd just had some fun now and then, it wouldn't have been all bottled up and ready to explode like that.'

'I didn't take a vow of celibacy. I just haven't met anybody else that...that spun my wheels enough.'

Because nobody had come close to being like Layla?

No. That was ridiculous. The world was full of gorgeous women. He just hadn't wanted the complications that came with even a brief entanglement. Work had been the answer. Satisfying enough, anyway.

Until now?

'Layla still spins them, then, I take it?' There was an odd note in Callie's voice. Wistful? No. More like resignation. This was more a sisterly thing. As though she was wanting to protect him from someone she knew had hurt him so much in the past.

'Obviously.' Alex's response was dry enough to evaporate instantly.

'Hmm. Well, at least it was just a quick shag in the shower. Nobody could say that was romantic.'

'No. I guess not.' Unbidden, images of Layla in a more romantic setting flashed into his head.

A big bed with rumpled sheets.

A soft rug in front of a crackling, open fire.

A candlelit dinner by a moon-touched sea.

Oh…God… It didn't matter that the images were so fleeting they almost hadn't touched his consciousness. They still left a drag of something way too close to longing in their wake.

He *didn't* want any of that. No way.

'And you didn't have a heart-to-heart and trot down memory lane?'

'We didn't get a chance to talk. The cops were waiting for us.'

'What? That was fast. How did they know what you'd been up to?'

Alex laughed and instantly felt better. Trust Callie to be able to break the tension like that. He filled her in on the incident with Ramona's boyfriend, which they'd managed to defuse completely with the solid wall of evidence from Cade, Layla and himself to refute the creep's claims that Alex had attacked him.

'And then I got caught up checking on Felix and by the time I'd finished, Layla had gone home so Cade and I went to O'Malley's for a drink.'

'Who's O'Malley?'

'It's an Irish pub. Close to Angel's so it gets used a

lot. You'd love it. Irish pubs are the same the world over. Could have been in O'Reilly's in Brisbane. Felt kind of like home, anyway.'

Except he didn't have a real home, did he? Never had. Maybe he never would. A shaft of a very melancholy shadow made him fall silent suddenly.

Callie didn't notice. 'And a good brotherly chat? You've really patched things up between you?'

'Yeah… Seems like it.' The shadow lifted. Maybe home was really about people, not places.

'So what did Cade have to say about you and Layla hooking up?'

'I…didn't get round to telling him about that.'

Callie made an impatient sound. '*Men*. What is with you and talking about personal stuff?'

'We talked about plenty of personal stuff.'

'Oh, yeah? Like what?'

'Cade's stuff.'

'Worse than yours?'

'Maybe.' Alex pressed his lips together. He wasn't about to break a confidence. And Cade's stuff had made him think his own worries were insignificant.

The worst that had happened to him had been that a girl he'd been crazy about had dumped him. She hadn't tried to trap him by getting pregnant and then punished him for not responding in the way she'd planned. Cade had had to deal with the guilt of this girl taking an overdose and then having a miscarriage.

'Anyway…' Callie had given up waiting for him to say anything more about the conversation. 'You working tomorrow?'

'It's Saturday and I'm not on call. I'll do a ward

round in the morning and was planning to catch up on paperwork after that.'

'Talk to Layla,' Callie ordered. 'If nothing else, you need to find out if she's on the Pill. Or whether you need to get screened for an STD or something.'

A curl of anger came from nowhere and was bright enough to make the night seem even hotter. 'Layla's not like that,' he snapped.

Why was the urge to protect her so automatic? What did he know about Layla these days? How on earth could he be so sure that he hadn't been put at risk despite doing something so irresponsible?

His rebuke had hit home. Callie sounded wary now. 'You still need to talk to her. Tomorrow. The longer you leave it, the harder it's going to be, and if you avoid her, you'll just be setting yourself up for another…um… shall we say, inappropriate means of dealing with the tension?'

A repeat of what had happened in the shower room? Oh…*yeah*…

Alex gave himself a firm mental shake. 'You're right. I'll catch her tomorrow and we'll talk about it. I'm sure she's as horrified as I am that it happened at all. Between us, we'll be able to figure out a way of making sure it doesn't happen again.'

'And…be careful, Alex.'

'How do you mean?'

'I'm not saying that Layla's not trustworthy or anything. Don't get me wrong, any woman that's managed to get under your skin the way she has must have a lot going for her. I'm just saying that maybe there's some merit in the whole "once bitten, twice shy" approach.'

Meaning he could get hurt. Again. As if he didn't know that.

'I get it,' he said softly. 'Thanks for caring, Cal.'

'No worries. Now, you need to get some sleep. What time is it over there?'

'Three a.m.' But Alex didn't want to end the call. Not while Callie was still sounding hurt by his defence of Layla's reputation. 'But I want to know how *you* are, Cal. How's it going at Gold Coast General?'

'Well…seeing as you've asked, I'm overworked and stressed out. If I don't get a new prenatal surgeon who's up to my impossibly high standards very soon, I will go stark raving mad.'

'Hmm.' Alex was only too happy to get completely distracted from his personal issues. He was also keen to do something to cheer Callie up. 'You know what? I might just be able to help you out there.'

'You're a neurosurgeon, Alex, not a prenatal surgeon.'

'True, but I might know one who could be interested.'

'Who? He'd have to be good.'

'He is. And I'm not just saying that because he's my brother.'

'You mean Cade? I thought he'd only just started at Angel's.'

'He has but he's finding it a bit frustrating. And I have to agree that he's too good to be second in charge. Funnily enough, he said something just the other day about thinking I had the right idea in going off to start a new life in Australia.'

With the benefit of hindsight, he could tell Cade that running away from some things didn't work. They could lie in wait for you and the ambush could be unexpected and very disturbing. He might be better to stay here and face his demons head on, if he had any. Except that maybe it *was* the answer for Cade.

Callie had picked up on his train of thought with her customary level of intuition.

'What's he running away from? If it's just his position on the ladder, there's nothing stopping him from finding a different hospital in the States.'

'Maybe he just needs to stretch his wings and see a bit of the world. He's young. Brilliant. Frustrated.'

'OK.' Callie was sounding much happier now. 'Tell me more, then. Just in case I need to talk to him.'

Finally, a puff of deliciously cool air came through the windows. Alex settled himself on the window sill. This was a conversation he was more than happy to have.

The one he would have to have tomorrow, with Layla?

Not so much. To put it mildly.


'Layla... Hey, wait up...'

'Chloe.'

The two women hugged each other in greeting. A paediatric nurse, Chloe Jenkins—no, Chloe Davis now that she'd married Brad—had been the first real friend Layla had made after arriving at Angel's.

'What's up?' Chloe pulled away to give Layla a questioning glance. 'You don't look like you're feeling great.'

'I'm just a bit tired.' Layla forced a smile. 'It was so hard to sleep last night with that heat. I need to ask my landlord to look at the air-conditioning unit.' She needed to change the subject quickly in case Chloe guessed she was trying to hide something. 'What are you doing in here on a Saturday morning when you're not on? I thought you and Brad were grabbing every chance you could get to go house hunting?'

'We are, but didn't you hear? Eleanor Aston had her baby last night.'

'Oh, wow…isn't that a bit early?'

'Yes, but they're both fine. Little girl. Tyler's over the moon.'

'I'll bet. What have they called her?'

Chloe laughed. 'I don't think they've decided. Right now, she's either "Peanut" or "Honey".'

'So Tyler's a daddy…' Layla shook her head. 'Astonishing.'

'Oh, that's right… You two go way back, don't you?'

'Since we were knee high to grasshoppers.' Layla was grinning now. 'I'll have to get him a cigar.'

'They might have chocolate ones in the gift shop. Come and have a look. That's why I'm here.' Chloe steered Layla across the lobby. 'I need to get a teddy bear or something before I go visiting and I've seen some really cute ones in our shop.'

'I've only got a minute. There's a queue of patients I need to catch up with this morning.'

'Must be a serious case amongst them.'

'Why do you say that?' Layla stopped beside a rack of cards. She could get one and send it to Eleanor and Tyler with Chloe.

'You look like you're on the way to give somebody some very bad news.'

'Oh…' Layla bit her lip. 'I guess I have got a conversation coming up that I'm not looking forward to.'

Chloe had reached out to pick up a teddy bear from

the shelf but her hand stopped in mid-air. 'I knew it. What's going on?'

Layla sighed. She picked up a card and pretended to read the message inside as she stepped closer to Chloe and lowered her voice enough to ensure she wasn't going to be overheard.

'You know how awkward it was seeing Brad at work after you two had slept together?'

'Do I ever. Oh, my God, Layla Woods.' Chloe's whisper became a gasp. 'Who *was* it?'

Layla was silent. Chloe's eyes widened.

'OK, you don't have to tell me because I can guess. It was Alex, wasn't it?'

It was Layla's turn to widen her eyes with shock.

'Don't worry.' Chloe touched her arm. 'It's not written all over your face or anything. I can guess because of the way I saw you two looking at each other when we had that girls' night out a while back.' She sucked in a deep breath. 'When did it happen?'

'Last night.' Layla felt the warmth of colour touching her cheeks. That was the only information she was about to share. Imagine if anybody heard about the actual circumstances? Oh...Lord...

'So what's the big deal?' Chloe picked up the bear and tested its cuddliness. 'You're single. So's he. He's *gorgeous*...and I'll bet the sex was...um...' she grinned mischievously '...memorable?'

'Oh, you have no idea,' Layla murmured. 'But it was a mistake. A big one.'

'Why?'

Why indeed?

Because they had to work together again now?

Because both of them were focussed so completely on their careers?

Because they had messed with each other's lives in the past so much they would never be able to trust each other?

That was more like it.

'Been there, done that,' Layla muttered. 'It wouldn't work.'

Chloe looked thoughtful. 'You can't know that for sure. If there's something there that's strong enough to pull you back together after...how many years?'

'Five.'

'Hmm. That's a pretty powerful something, if you ask me. Does Alex think it was a big mistake?'

'I don't know. We haven't talked about it.'

'Oh...' Chloe's grimace was sympathetic. 'No wonder it's awkward. Good luck with that.'

'Thanks. I think I'm going to need it.'

# CHAPTER FIVE

IT WAS LATER on that Saturday morning before Alex and Layla saw each other and when they did, it was so much like a stand-off in some old Western movie that Layla almost laughed aloud.

She'd stepped out of the elevator on the eighth floor with the intention of going into the neurology ward and finding Alex. She had expected to see him so she shouldn't have been so surprised. What she hadn't expected was to find him striding towards the elevators. That was why her breath caught in her throat and why her heart rate suddenly accelerated. Why her feet seemed to be glued to the floor.

Alex had stopped dead in his tracks with the double doors of the ward entrance still swinging gently behind him.

They were both frozen.

Who's going to reach for their gun first? Layla wondered. Her lips twitched at the ridiculousness of this and, with a determined inward shove she started moving. So did Alex.

Not exactly towards each other. By a kind of telepathic tacit consent they both moved in a V-shaped track that brought them together close to the big windows.

The view over Central Park from this height was spectacular. You could see from the park's southern border almost as far as the huge reservoir in the northern half of this massive area. Layla stared down at the park rather than directly at Alex.

'Gorgeous day, isn't it?'

'Mmm.' It felt like Alex was staring at her rather than the view. Layla's heart skipped a beat. She knew they needed to talk about what had happened last night but she wasn't ready. Nowhere near ready. She could feel her heart skip a beat and she had to dampen her suddenly dry lips.

'I love this end of the park,' she said brightly. 'It's got the best bits. I just love the bird sanctuary and the zoo and…and the sheep meadow.'

Oh, good grief…the sheep meadow? It was nothing more than a vast grassy space where people had picnics or threw Frisbees.

Alex cleared his throat. 'The lake would be a nice spot on a warm day like this.' His hesitation was almost imperceptible. 'Got time for a walk?'

'Um…yeah, I guess.' Layla risked a quick glance at Alex, wishing her heart rate would settle. It was crazy to be feeling this nervous. 'I've only got a bit of paperwork waiting for me and it'll still be waiting when I get back.'

'Same.' Alex met her glance briefly and Layla realised he was as nervous as she was about having this conversation. Was that why he was suggesting they have it well away from the place they both worked?

Oddly, the fact that Alex was nervous calmed Layla enough to make her smile. 'I could kill for a hot dog or something,' she said. 'I'm *starving*.'

A wash of surprise, or maybe relief, crossed Alex's features.

'Same.'

'Let's get out of here, then.' Layla led the way.

They had to share the elevator with a troupe of candy-stripers heading off to the cafeteria for lunch. If Alex was remotely aware of the increase in the amount of giggling and the eyelashes that got batted in his direction, he gave no indication of it.

The lobby was crowded with people. Weekends were a time when lots of visitors could get to Angel's and often there were special treats planned for the young patients. Today it looked as if a celebrity basketball player was making an appearance and he was being tailed by a television crew.

Alex and Layla still hadn't spoken another word to each other by the time they emerged from the front entrance of Angel's into the welcome fresh air and sunshine. Walking side by side, Layla turned her head as they passed the small statue.

Alex noticed the movement. 'You know who that is?' he asked.

'I got told by the taxi driver who dropped me here when I came for the job interview. It's Angel Mendez, a little boy who died of polio during the Great Depression. That's where the hospital got its name.'

'Did you know that his dad was a paediatrician?' Alex asked.

'No. I hadn't heard that bit. How tragic that he couldn't save his own son.'

'His name was Federico Mendez. He wanted to honour Angel's memory and try and make sure other parents didn't lose their kids. This was New York's first free children's hospital.'

'It's a great history.' Layla couldn't help reaching out to brush the statue with her fingers as she passed. She was by no means the only person who ever did that. The bronze of this much-loved statue had weathered to a greenish tinge but the hands of the small boy were shiny because they were on a level that could be touched. By adults like her, or by children being lifted up or climbing so that they could make contact with something they could identify with.

'Mmm.' Alex was a little ahead of her now. 'Kind of sums up what we're all about, doesn't it?'

The road in front of them was wide and busy. Ambulances were turning into the hospital grounds and yellow cabs were sprinkled thickly amongst the heavy traffic. A police car went by with its lights and siren blaring. Alex led the way as the lights changed. A horse-drawn carriage was turning into the park and open-topped, double-decker tourist buses were offloading passengers.

'Which way? Right to the bird sanctuary or left to the lake?'

'The lake,' Layla said. The draw of water in the middle of a late summer's day was irresistible.

So was the smell of hot food from the carts as they walked through the crowds in the shade of the big old trees. Layla shook her head at someone trying to sell her a balloon and at someone else who wanted her to buy a walking guide to the park but she couldn't go past a cart selling Mexican food.

'Nachos,' she breathed. 'My favourite. Even better

than a hot dog.' She smiled winningly up at Alex. 'Do you mind waiting?'

He didn't seem to mind. In fact, the corners of his eyes crinkled as he smiled back. 'Go right ahead. I'll go and grab a burger from that cart we just passed. Meet you back here in five minutes.'

They kept walking after buying their food and drink because it wasn't far to the lake now. And then they sat and ate under the shady trees, watching people in rowboats and elegant swans floating past. A group of hungry ducks emerged from the water to watch them eat.

'No way,' Layla told them. 'You wouldn't like corn chips, anyway.'

She scooped another mouthful of savoury beans and cheese into her mouth and closed her eyes from the sheer pleasure of it all. Then she opened them and blinked. She was enjoying this?

The cloud of the conversation she and Alex had to have was still there but, again by some unspoken agreement, they were putting it off until they'd eaten. For the moment this felt remarkably like…well…a *date*.

Here she was, in a gorgeous setting on a stunning day, having a meal in the company of the most attractive man she'd ever known.

What had Chloe said? He was single. So was she.

There was something between them that was clearly strong enough to pull them together again with the force of an overstretched rubber band being released.

Was it even remotely possible that they could make a fresh start?

Would she *want* to?

Layla found herself watching Alex as he broke a piece off his hamburger bun and held it out. A brave duck was edging closer, gathering the courage to snatch the morsel from those long, surgeon's fingers. But Layla's gaze travelled up his arm to where his shirtsleeve was rolled up far enough to show the bulge of muscle in his upper arm.

The skin was dry now, of course, but Layla could still see it glistening with the drops of water from his shower last night. And she knew exactly what that bunch of muscle would feel like if she gripped it really tightly.

Oh...yes...

She would want to.

The duck who was brave enough to take bread from his fingers probably wasn't expecting his friends to turn on him the instant he succeeded. The cacophony of quacking and the violent flapping of so many wings broke the peaceful, summer picnic vibe that Alex had been enjoying more than he was prepared to acknowledge.

Late summer suited Layla. The sunlight made her blonde hair glow golden and she still managed to look smart in her light clothing. The skirt that swirled around her bare legs. The soft-looking shirt that had rolled-up sleeves fastened with a little tab and button and was unbuttoned down the front so it was like a jacket over a camisole top that clung to her curves and had an eye-catching bit of beadwork around that hint of cleavage.

Those bare legs were stuck out in front of her as she sat on the grass, licking melted cheese and salsa off her fingers with a totally unselfconscious enjoyment of her food. The skin on her calves looked tanned and smooth but Alex had been successfully resisting the urge to touch them because he knew that, however smooth the bits on show were, they couldn't compete with the skin hidden beneath the folds of that pretty skirt.

Yeah. It was just as well the duck fight broke the spell and reminded him of the intended purpose of this outing. It wasn't a date. Somehow they had to clear the air and sort out a way of being able to work together.

Alex sat up from where he'd been lounging on the grass propped up on one elbow. He took a deep breath and turned to look directly at Layla, wondering just how to start this conversation.

She caught his glance and he could see the way she caught her breath. She knew what was coming and she was nervous about it.

Why? Why was *he* so nervous, for that matter? They had a common goal here. They both wanted the same thing, didn't they? Maybe Layla simply wasn't ready to talk yet. Not about the big stuff, anyway.

'I saw Mike Jenner this morning,' she told him. 'Tommy's dad. He and Gina had brought Tommy in to get the pre-admission tests done. I didn't realise that Monday's the big day.'

Alex made a noncommittal sound. Why would she? Tommy Jenner was his patient, not Layla's.

Except that the little boy's case had captured the imagination of the entire staff at Angel's once the story had got round of how close a call it had been for his father to be accused of abuse. And of how serious Tommy's condition was. Any kid with a brain tumour was enough to tug at the heart strings but this one was definitely special.

'Mike's really stressed,' Layla continued. 'Which was why he was so keen to talk, I think. There's so much riding on this.'

Alex could feel an unpleasant kind of pressure himself. Of course there was a lot riding on this. A little boy's life.

'He wants to ask Gina to marry him,' Layla said quietly into the silence. 'But it's not the right time. If things go well, then he can see it being part of the celebration later. A new future for Tommy. A new family. It's lovely, isn't it? That Mike and Gina found each other in the midst of all that worry and that they both love Tommy so much?'

Still Alex couldn't say anything. He didn't need to be hearing this. Didn't want the feeling of emotional blackmail that could colour the huge decision he had to make on Monday about whether or not to go ahead with the complicated surgery.

'It's just as well they have each other.' Layla sounded as if she was talking to herself as the soft words continued to spill out. 'How awful would it be when you have to pin the hopes for your future on a decision that would mean your baby had to undergo such a risky operation?'

And then, as though the implications of her words were only now sinking in, Layla ducked her head and bit her lip.

'Sorry...' she muttered. 'I...get a bit carried away, don't I?'

'No kidding.' Alex spoke more sharply than he'd intended. 'Surely you're experienced enough by now to know how unwise it is to get too emotionally involved in a case?'

'It's never unwise to *care*,' Layla retorted.

A bubble of something hot and nasty was expanding in his gut. Anger that was encased in a skin of confusion.

He didn't get it.

Layla had always become too emotionally involved. He'd seen that when they'd first met over Jamie Kirkpatrick's case—the little boy whose condition was eerily similar to Tommy's. She was so passionate about her job. Cared so intensely about her patients and their families.

And yet she could dump someone she was in a relationship with without so much as a second thought. Without even looking back to see what kind of damage she'd done.

Without *caring*.

'I'll make my decisions based on my professional expertise,' Alex said coldly. 'I'll look at the results of the MRI on Monday and judge whether the chemo has made enough of a difference to improve the odds of attempting a surgery that has the very real risk of ending Tommy's life immediately.'

The bubble was getting bigger. It wouldn't take much to burst it.

'I do not need anybody telling me just how much the future happiness of his father depends on the outcome,' he continued. 'I will make a rational, *professional* choice about the actions I take.'

'Oh...?' Layla's hands were curled into fists and her voice was laced with derision. 'Like you did last night, do you mean?'

OK, that did it. This might not be the way into that conversation that he'd anticipated but he wasn't about to hold back now. Except that Layla got in another barb first.

'Do you make a habit of having unprotected sex?'

'No.' Alex spoke through gritted teeth. 'Do *you*?'

Layla gave an incredulous huff. 'The last person I had sex with, other than my *husband*,' she hissed, 'was *you*.'

Alex had only just started to form a coherent train of thought through the mist of red-hot anger. Now he was stunned into silence again. How long had Layla been divorced? There hadn't been anyone since?

*Why not?*

'So you don't need to worry that you've caught any-thing unpleasant,' Layla went on scathingly. 'And I'm not pregnant. If I hadn't been right at the end of my cycle I would have taken a morning-after pill today.'

The clinical delivery of the information was chill-ingly impersonal. Alex couldn't meet the glare he knew was coming in his direction. He stared straight ahead. The ducks, realising that any prospect of food was gone, were filing back into the lake. In search of a more con-genial atmosphere?

'You don't need to worry either,' he told Layla stiffly. 'The only relationship I've had in the last five years was way back when I first arrived in Brisbane. I've been tested and cleared of any transmittable diseases since then, thanks to having to work as a surgeon.'

He could actually feel Layla digesting that startling piece of information.

There was a long, long silence. He could feel her cu-riosity building. He might be wondering himself why Layla was still single but he wouldn't ask her straight out. Layla wouldn't shy away from something like that, though. She just wouldn't be able to help herself.

Sure enough, she asked, albeit a tad hesitantly.

'Why not?'

Alex shrugged. 'Too busy,' he said, with an attempt at lightness. 'You know how it is.'

'Yeah…' The agreement encompassed something a lot bigger than a busy career. She knew.

Alex shot her a glance. 'And maybe I'm too well aware of the damage that emotional involvement causes. Professional *and* personal.'

Another silence. And then Layla sighed and the sound was like an admission of defeat.

'I'm sorry,' she said quietly.

'What for?'

'The…way things ended. That whole mess. I didn't think for a moment that anything would go wrong with Jamie's operation and that made it all so much worse.'

'Not for you.' Alex didn't care what the bitter words might reveal. 'You just walked away without a backward glance. *I* was the one who got slapped with a malpractice suit. *I* was the one left wondering if my unprofessional involvement with a colleague had somehow undermined my ability to do my job well enough.'

'You think I didn't feel guilty?' Layla whispered. Her voice rose. 'I was *married*, for God's sake, Alex. My life was falling apart.'

Alex had to get to his feet. How dared she suggest that that black time had been just as bad for her as it had been for him? He jammed his hands in his pockets and took a few jerky steps towards the lake. Then he whirled back to face Layla.

'So why the hell did you get tangled up with me in the first place, then?'

She looked…anguished. Her voice came out sounding as though she might start crying.

Layla Woods crying? Unthinkable.

'Probably for the same reason that last night happened,' she said, jerking her head sideways as she stopped speaking, as though it was taking an enormous physical effort to break the eye contact with him.

So she hadn't wanted it to happen? Simply hadn't been able to resist, despite knowing that it was, somehow, so wrong? There was a world of unspoken pain hidden beneath those quiet words.

Alex had to exert the same kind of physical effort he'd seen Layla display. To stop himself moving forward. Reaching for Layla's hands to pull her to her feet. So that he could wrap his arms around her.

And hold her.

The silence around them was broken by the far-away sound of children laughing and the much closer sound of a rowboat near the shore of the lake, the oars dipping and splashing. The sound make Alex think of more than water.

Of wet skin.

The slide of bodies that couldn't get close enough fast enough.

Layla was getting to her feet but she didn't come any closer. She just stared at Alex.

'It happened,' she said steadily. 'The point is, what are we going to do about it?'

He swore softly, under his breath. She was right. There was a physical attraction between them that was irresistible.

So powerful it had the potential to destroy them both.

'I don't know,' he said, his voice catching. 'I really don't know.'

Layla held his gaze. 'Neither do I.'

This was a standoff of a very different kind from the

one Layla had been aware of when she'd stepped out of the elevator on the eighth floor of Angel's a couple of hours ago.

This one wasn't funny at all.

'Do we just walk away?' Alex suggested. 'Pretend it never happened?'

He still hadn't broken that intense gaze that was locked with her own. No. They both knew that wasn't going to happen.

'There's another way we could deal with it,' Layla heard herself saying cautiously.

A tiny flash of interest—hope, maybe—brightened the dark gaze in front of her. 'Which is?'

'Um… There's some kind of a spark between us, isn't there?'

A huff of breath from Alex. Something halfway between a snort of laughter and a groan.

'And being around each other is kind of like having a pile of fuel available.'

Alex was silent but he was listening. Carefully.

'Sometimes…' Layla swallowed hard '…if you throw the fuel onto the spark and make a fire, the fuel runs out and the fire just…goes out by itself.'

She could see Alex processing the idea. His face went very still.

What was he thinking? Did he feel the *shower* of sparks Layla could feel dancing in the air between them? And the certain knowledge that the tiniest bit of fuel, in the form of a kiss maybe, would ignite those sparks into the hottest flames imaginable. And that those flames could be healing. They could burn away the resentment and mistrust that lay between them after the way they'd parted five years ago.

'Is that what you want to do?' His voice was the rawest sound Layla had ever heard.

She couldn't say a word.

All she could do was hold his gaze, knowing that he would see her answer in her face.

She saw his chest expand as he sucked in a huge breath. Saw the way he dampened his bottom lip with his tongue and the sparks got so bright her vision blurred.

'It could work,' he added, as they both began moving, the spell that had held them so still now broken. 'But fire's a dangerous thing to play around with. There's a risk that someone could get badly burned.'

Layla nodded, far more slowly this time. It would probably be her, she thought.

Did she really want to put herself in such a vulnerable position?

*Yes...*

The tiny voice was remarkably decisive.

Because there was just a chance, wasn't there?

A chance that the fuel wouldn't run out completely. That the huge flames would burn with a blinding brightness but then settle and leave a glow that might...just *might*...be enough.

And if she didn't take that chance, she might regret it for the rest of her life.

# CHAPTER SIX

LAYLA ARRIVED AT work on Monday morning as nervous as a long-tailed cat in a room full of rocking chairs.

Yesterday had to have been the longest day in her life.

The longest night, anyway.

What had she expected? That Alex would give it some thought, decide that it was a good idea to see if they could deal with their lingering attraction by indulging it and then be unable to wait another night until they could put the plan into action?

Yeah…maybe she had and that was why she'd been waiting for her phone to ring or, at least for a text message signal to sound.

Why her heart had leapt into her throat when her ringtone broke the increasingly tense silence of her Sunday evening.

Talking to her mother was the same as always. Gully-washing October rain had set in. Her father was planning to run for yet another term as mayor. Her ex-husband, Luke, was going to be a father again and there was even a whisper about town that it might be twins this time. Fortunately, the topic of conversation Celia Woods was most concerned about was how she was going to provide the best treats in town for the children who would come knocking on Halloween.

'I don't know, Momma.' If she was honest, Layla didn't actually care. Halloween traditions were the last thing on her mind right now but this was preferable to being reminded of the life she could have had if she'd stayed with Luke. 'Why don't you do some of those meringue ghosts or the cat-shaped cookies you did one year? They look pretty special when you wrap them up in Cellophane and ribbons. Can't you get food dye that makes things black now?'

'I do believe you can. That's a real good idea, honey. I'm gonna go and fix my shopping list right now.'

The silence seemed even heavier after that phone call.

Nothing changed in Swallow Creek and suddenly that was making Layla feel even more on edge about what was happening in her life. The new life she had come here to start. One that had been so full of promise.

One that she had just lobbed a grenade into and now she was waiting to see if Alex was going to pull the pin.

Maybe it would be better if he didn't.

And how long was she going to have to wait to find out? Mondays were always hectic. Surgery lists would be jam-packed and weekends had the habit of accumulating issues that could wait until somebody senior enough was available to make decisions.

Layla was caught up in meetings, one of which was with the committee dedicated to raising the funds for a new MRI machine. The meeting had barely started, however, before she received an urgent summons to the emergency department.

And that was when her day started to go downhill.

Not that she realised it at the time, but it took another dive when she sent someone to page Alex with an even more urgent summons than the one she'd received.

It should have been Ryan O'Doherty that Layla had summoned because the deputy head of the neurology department was on call for emergency cases today. Alex had arrived with the intention of telling Layla that but one look at the determined set of her mouth and he knew he wasn't going to be permitted to delegate.

'I need the very best surgeon we've got,' she said.

Was this some kind of play to weld something personal into the professional? Had Layla done her own thinking and second-guessed the decision Alex had come to last night? Was this was a clever counter-offensive to make him change his mind? Now certainly wasn't the time to set her straight but he couldn't leave it much longer.

Taking a closer look, Alex could see that the fierce passion making those blue eyes glow so brightly was purely professional. Layla had no head room for any kind of personal agenda right now. This was all about a six-year-old boy called Matthew.

Alex had perched one hip on the edge of the desk in the office Layla had commandeered in the ER. 'Fill me in.'

'I met Matthew four months ago. It was my first outpatient clinic day during my orientation week. He was in the waiting room with his mother, Dayna. She's a single mum. Matthew's father was killed in an industrial accident before she even knew she was pregnant.'

Alex was tempted to tell Layla to cut to the chase. The medical details. But the words were spilling out with wobbly edges and she was using her hands a lot while she talked. This was pure Layla. The story of any patient had to include a picture of the whole person. He needed to be patient and simply listen for a minute because she was going to tell him the story whether he liked it or not.

'He'd found a toy aeroplane in the basket. One of those double-winged ones, you know? Like Snoopy uses when he's being the Red Baron?'

Alex felt one side of his mouth curl upwards and his impatience faded as he listened to the lilt in Layla's voice that always got stronger when she was passionate about something. He watched the emotions that flitted across her face and was reminded of what an extraordinary woman she was. Unique. If he could somehow distance himself enough to become merely a good friend, her company would be a joy.

'There was a battle going on. The Red Baron was gaining height, ready to dive-bomb something. Possibly his mother's foot because she was busy reading a magazine and wasn't paying enough attention to the battle. Anyway...I came round the corner and there was a...a mid-air incident and the Red Baron crashed into my leg.'

Alex's lips twitched. He could imagine the scene.

'Fortunately there were no major injuries but poor Dayna was mortified when she found me sitting in with the consultant when she came in with Matthew for his appointment. I told her it was a real joy to see one of our cardiology patients looking so healthy. Matthew was in for a five-year check because he'd been a patient at Angel's when he was a baby to have a major vascular anomaly corrected.'

Alex finally frowned. 'This is a cardiology case? Why the hell have you called me down here? I'm in the middle of—'

Layla held up her hand, cutting him off.

'Dayna asked for me when she brought Matthew into Emergency this morning, maybe because she remembered the way we'd met. She'd found Mattie banging his head on the floor of the bathroom 'because it hurt so much'. He vomited twice and was found to have neck stiffness and photophobia on arrival.'

Alex's frown deepened. 'Sounds like meningitis.'

'Spinal tap was negative. We wondered about a head trauma after that so we got a CT scan done.'

'And?' Alex had closed his eyes for a moment. He did not need another case like Tommy Jenner. A brain lesion in a small child that Layla cared about a little too much. Then his eyes snapped open. This was worse, wasn't it?

'A major cardiac vascular anomaly as a baby? He's got a cerebral aneurysm, hasn't he?'

Layla nodded, her face now a picture of misery. 'Dayna's beside herself. She thought they'd got through the worst that life had to throw at both her and Mattie. He's started school now and he's such a happy kid. He…he told me he's going to be a fighter pilot when he grows up.'

Oh…*hell*…

'You'd better show me the CT.' Alex knew he sounded cool and distant but he'd been sucked in, hadn't he? Lulled by watching and listening to Layla and now he had more involvement on an emotional level than he was comfortable with before he'd even met the patient.

And there would be no luxury of time to consider a decision here, like he'd had with Tommy. The CT results were crystal clear. The damaged vessel in Matthew's brain was at risk of bursting at any moment and the results would be catastrophic. Severe brain injury. Or death. The surgery could be equally catastrophic but it was his only chance.

Could Ryan perform this surgery? Yes. Did Alex want to pass it on? He *could* use his position as head of department and say that Ryan needed the experience of this case.

Layla had remained silent while Alex studied the CT scan images. She stood back when he went to meet Dayna and Matthew. Small for his age, Matthew had a very pale face, big brown eyes and spiky black hair. He was in pain and terrified.

'Hey, buddy…' Alex could feel something squeeze hard in his chest when he smiled gently at the little boy. 'I hear you're going to be a fighter pilot when you grow up?'

Huge brown eyes were locked on his face. He heard the suppressed sob that came from Matthew's mother, who was sitting beside the bed, holding her son's hand. And he could feel Layla's watchful gaze from somewhere behind him. Could feel the *hope*.

'I've heard that there's a special airplane bed somewhere around here,' he told Matthew. 'What say I arrange for you to fly upstairs to come and have the operation to fix that nasty headache you've got?'

He had to brush close to Layla as he went ahead to set things up. He hadn't expected her to follow him. He didn't want to see the gratitude in her eyes when she touched his arm and forced him to stop just as he got to the internal double doors of the emergency room.

'Thanks,' she whispered.

'Don't thank me.' Alex knew he sounded curt but he couldn't let this go on. 'This isn't anything personal, Layla.' He held her gaze and had the odd sensation that he was trying to use his own to push her as far away as possible. 'I've thought about it,' he added, 'and the answer's no. We're colleagues now. And that's all we can be. Anything else is a recipe for disaster.'

He saw the shock of his words but he had to hand it to Layla. If she was disappointed she hid it completely.

'You're probably right,' was all she said. 'I'd better get back to Matthew. Maybe I can catch you later to follow up.' She turned away. 'On the surgery, I mean.'

Alex pushed the doors open with a little more force than necessary. *Probably* right? What did that mean? And had she really needed to underline that talking to him later would be purely professional?

Hell…maybe she wasn't disappointed at all.

Scrubbing in for Matthew's surgery a commendably short time later should have been the end of any personal undercurrents in Alex's thoughts. This was always a private time when he could centre himself and focus completely on what was going to happen when he had finished this intensive preparation.

Except it was taking a lot longer than usual to get to that focussed space. The suds being formed by the small soap-impregnated scrubbing brush foamed all over his hands but he wasn't ready to rinse them off.

He kept scrubbing. Under each fingernail. In the webbing between each finger. In a world of his own during this automatic preparation for surgery.

When you looked back on your life, he found himself musing, sometimes it's easy to see a particular day that marked a turning point in your life.

He'd had quite a few of them.

Like that dreadful day when he'd been only ten years old, and his beloved mother had died of breast cancer.

The day he'd finally walked out on his abusive step-father, when he'd been sixteen, having made the heart-breaking decision that it would be better for Cade if he removed himself from the picture.

The day he'd first set eyes on Layla Woods and had realised that, against all the odds, he *was* still capable of trusting someone else.

Of loving them.

The flow of warm water was like balm after all that scrubbing. Alex rinsed the foam off his hands and then changed the angle of his arms so that he could rinse from his wrists to his elbows without letting the foam touch the well-cleaned skin of his hands. He picked up the sterile towel to dry himself, still lost in his thoughts.

In a few seconds he knew he would be able to turn them off as decisively as the tap he'd just been using and focus with the same intensity on the job ahead of him, but he also knew that, to get to that point of focus, he needed to let this train of thought reach its conclusion.

None of those earlier, turning-point days had been clearly marked in advance so that you got the chance to think about it and weigh up the potential benefits and downsides. Like he had been able to do ever since he'd parted company from Layla after their time in Central Park. Ever since he'd seen that willingness in Layla's eyes to start something between them again.

The history he had with both Callie and Cade would colour whatever advice they might give him. The his-tory he had with Layla made it impossible to think rationally when he was close to her, let alone talk to her and hear that sweet Texan drawl that had been one of the first things that had attracted him to her.

By late Sunday night Alex had decided that getting back into any kind of a relationship with Layla would be a bad idea. He'd been quite confident that, with the calming distraction of a heavy day at work, that decision would seat itself so firmly he would be more than ready to talk to Layla later and find another way to deal with having to work together.

He was still confident that the decision was right. He just hadn't bargained on this turning out to be such a stressful day.

OK, he'd known that making a decision about Tommy Jenner would be a tough call and his heart had sunk as he'd watched the MRI images coming up on screen this morning. The call was too close to make one way or the other right now. A professional and emotional tightrope. The hardest thing had been to face Mike and Gina in his office and tell them he needed more time. That, despite their desperate pleas, he couldn't tell them his decision until he'd given it a lot more thought.

And it had been at the end of that interview that he'd received the summons to join Layla in the emergency department.

Well…he'd told her his decision now. And she'd accepted it.

The worst was over.

Now he could focus properly and move on. Do what he did best and go into Theatre to try and save a young life.

* * *

Layla slipped into the observation area above the operating theatre.

She saw the busy team preparing the theatre around the tiny, still form that was Matthew lying there under the bright lights. The television screen up here showed a close-up of Matthew's head. A large patch of his adorable, spiky hair had been shaved off and a nurse was painting the skin with iodine.

She saw the moment the star of the show arrived, hands held carefully crossed in front of his body, using his shoulder blade to bump open the swing doors that separated the theatre from the scrubbing-in area.

*Alex...*

He could do this. He could save Mattie. Layla's teeth sank into her bottom lip so hard it hurt. It didn't matter about the decision Alex had come to regarding what they did about the attraction they had for each other. All that mattered in this moment was the life of the child on the table.

*Please...*

As if he felt the force of her plea, Alex looked up as he took his position at the head of the operating table. Layla was by no means alone in the observation area but his gaze went unswervingly to where she was sitting.

Could he actually see her face behind the wall of glass when the lights down there were so much brighter?

Possibly not. But he was aware of her, that was for sure.

Layla's heart gave a painful thump. Maybe she shouldn't be here. Could her presence, reminding him of the tension between them, distract him in any way?

The way she'd always believed it had in Jamie Kirk-patrick's case?

She'd put pressure on him back then, ending their affair.

She'd put pressure on him again now, suggesting that they revisit that affair as a way of dealing with their un-finished business.

If anything bad happened to Matthew today, that would be the end. Alex would never want anything to do with her again.

Had she realised how much she was putting on the line by insisting that Alex get involved with this case? Had she even thought that he might take the opportu-nity to get what he wanted to say over with?

Of course she hadn't. She had followed her heart.

The disappointment of hearing his decision had been a body blow that she was still reeling from but Layla was fighting back. She *shouldn't* be this disappointed. She'd never expected to have Alex Rodriguez back in her professional environment, let alone her personal life.

Why couldn't she learn not to be so impulsive? To take the time to really weigh up the repercussions of making emotionally based decisions? She'd done this too many times in her life already.

Like when she'd fallen into Alex's arms in the first place, all those years ago.

When she'd ended things between them because she hadn't been able to stand the guilt and the way he had been making her feel.

When she'd practically thrown herself at Alex and suggested they kept seeing each other. Intimately.

The emotional overload was unbearable but, thankfully, it coalesced into only an imperceptible moment in time.

The subtle nod that came from Alex was probably just as imperceptible to anyone other than Layla. He seemed to be acknowledging her presence.

And reassuring her that it wouldn't distract him.

The whole team was poised as Alex turned his attention to the exposed patch of Matthew's head. He held out his hand.

'Scalpel.'

The critical point of this surgery came when the blood supply to the brain had to be compromised to allow a permanent repair to the damaged vessel, which was a major artery. There was only a small window of time— four minutes—before the blood flow had to be fully restored to avoid the certainty of brain damage. If the repair hadn't been done well enough by then, there would be no second chances.

'Start the clock.'

The order was delivered with crisp precision.

Alex was ready.

A small boy's life depended on what he was about to do. The child's desperate mother was sitting in a waiting room not far away. Layla was sitting in the observation area of this operating theatre.

Part of Alex's brain was aware of all these things and their implications but none of them could even begin to intrude on his intense focus on the job in hand. The intricate and challenging clipping of this defective blood vessel without allowing it to burst or cause any collateral damage through the technique.

The clock kept ticking.

'Two minutes,' the anaesthetist warned.

Beads of perspiration formed on Alex's forehead. A nurse patted them dry with a gauze swab. He had to blink and refocus his vision through the magnifying lenses of his eyewear.

The clip was so tiny. Slippery. So hard to slip into exactly the right position and keep it there long enough to secure it.

'Fifty-eight seconds,' the anaesthetist said quietly. 'Forty-five...thirty...'

It was there. In place. Alex squeezed it shut.

'Stop the clock.'

Another minute of complete silence as Alex inspected his handiwork in minute detail and finally he could give the verdict that created a collective release of breaths being held.

'Looking good. We can close up now.'

It was done and he knew it had been done well.

Only now could Alex allow himself a split second of satisfaction before focussing on the automatic protocols of closing. A moment to take a deeper breath and know that he had made a difference. Saved a life?

Quite possibly, although there was still plenty to be anxious about until he could measure the steps to recovery that Matthew would need to take.

Still, he could look forward to telling Dayna that the surgery had gone as well as they could have hoped for.

He could imagine what he would see in Layla's eyes when they next came face to face.

Gratitude, for sure. Far more than he'd seen when he'd agreed to take on this surgery in the first place.

Admiration as well?

The bone flap was back in place in Matthew's skull

a short time later and the probe to measure intracranial pressure was secured and tested. The final stitches and bandaging were the only tasks to be completed. Alex could relax.

And it was then that the realisation hit him.

He had been aware of the undercurrent of emotional pressure of this surgery, not only for his patient and the family but from Layla's investment in this case. From having her right there, watching his every move.

And it hadn't made any difference. He had put it aside and done exactly what he'd needed to do, to the very best of his ability.

Maybe he could handle more than he'd thought he was capable of when it came to Layla.

If he was aware of the danger of real emotional involvement, he could overcome it. Just like he'd just demonstrated when he'd been concentrating on Matthew's operation.

If he heeded Callie's warning, he could make sure he didn't start trusting Layla too much. So that when the end came, as it would, he would be prepared for it and it wouldn't destroy him because he would have been in control all along.

Maybe Layla had been right all along.

If they threw fuel on the smouldering ashes of what had once burned so brightly between them, it could burn itself out for once and for all.

It had worked with Callie Richards, hadn't it?

And if it could burn itself out, he wouldn't be left for the rest of his life wondering what if...?

No wonder last night's decision had been so hard won.

It had been the wrong choice.

But he'd already told Layla so it was too late to change his mind.

Or was it?

As the final stitch was cut, Alex dropped the curved needle and its holder onto the instrument trolley and looked up to where Layla had been sitting at the end of the row of seats. As soon as he saw her again, he might know the answer to that burning little question.

The seat was empty now. Layla wasn't there.

Layla had slipped out of the observation area with much the same stealth as she'd entered it, only this time she was having to swallow past a painful constriction in her throat.

She was just so darned *proud* of Alex.

Not that she could tell him that. She needed to clear her head and get back into a space where she could tell him how well he'd done on a strictly professional level without revealing such a personal response. He wouldn't want to see that. It would spell the end of being able to work together without the kind of tension that would inevitably become too poisonous to be tolerable.

Keeping herself busy, Layla waited a couple of hours before going to the PICU herself, where she found Matthew resting comfortably, still well sedated, and Dayna exhausted but with her eyes still bright with tears of relief.

'Dr Rodriguez is brilliant, isn't he?'

'He sure is.'

'He said we won't know if there's been any lasting damage until Mattie's properly awake again. That he might have some hurdles with his speech for a while, or a weakness on one side. But that he's young enough to recover completely from anything like that and that it was so lucky we found the problem in time.'

'I'm so happy we did.' Layla shared a hug with Dayna. 'I'll come by and see how you're both doing again tomorrow morning.' She stood back to cast a practised eye over the monitors surrounding Matthew's bed and Dayna followed the direction of her searching gaze.

'Dr Rodriguez said it's all looking real good. You just missed him. He said he had to go and check on another patient on the ward. That it seemed to be his day for special little boys who needed big operations.'

Layla caught her breath.

Tommy.

Alex must have gone to give his decision to Mike and Gina about whether or not he would operate. She knew how big a decision that would have been to make because she'd seen those MRI results.

The tumour had shrunk thanks to the chemotherapy but it was still a nasty one and it was in a very difficult spot. Uncannily like the one Jamie Kirkpatrick had had.

She could understand if that was enough to make Alex shy away from the challenge but would it have made any difference, having had the success with Matthew today?

Layla had to find out. This wasn't personal so she had no trouble justifying the need to see him. She didn't even give herself the time to question the wisdom of doing so.

She went straight from the PICU to the neurology ward. To Alex's office.

The door was very slightly ajar and she could see the screen on the wall with an image from an MRI being displayed. Tommy's MRI.

Did he still have Mike and Gina in the office? She couldn't hear the sound of any voices but could they be sitting in stunned silence trying to absorb some very bad news?

No. Alex would have closed his door before having a conversation like that.

Indecisiveness was not an option here. Layla tapped lightly on the door and went in, pushing the door shut quietly behind her.

Alex was alone in his office. Standing by the window, clearly lost in thought, tapping the end of the ballpoint pen he was holding against his bottom lip. Papers were strewn across his desk and some of them had rough-looking sketches. The kind you might make if you were talking someone through what was going to happen in a complex operation.

Alex turned slowly to watch Layla as she looked up from noting the sketches.

'You're going to do it?' she asked softly. 'Tommy's operation?'

The response was a curt nod. 'Everybody understands the risks.'

'But it's worth a shot?'

Another nod. More considered this time. Alex was holding her gaze and Layla could see something that had nothing to do with any patient in his eyes. She had to take in a slow, steadying breath. What she was seeing now was very, very different from the way he'd looked at her when he'd told her his decision.

He looked as if…as if he'd changed his mind.

'What about us, Alex?' The words came out as a whisper. 'Do you really think we're not worth a shot too?'

For a long, long moment Alex didn't move a muscle. Didn't make a sound.

He took a step towards her. The ballpoint pen clattered onto the surface of his desk.

And then he took Layla in his arms and she closed her eyes as her head tilted back under the pressure of his lips on hers.

It seemed like she had her answer.

# CHAPTER SEVEN

SOMETHING WAS VERY different this time.

Giving in to the overwhelming attraction between them had always been illicit. Tinged with the knowledge that it was dangerous. That somebody was going to get hurt.

That it was *wrong*.

Even the other night, when Alex had been blindsided by Layla appearing in the decontamination shower, the encounter had been just as illicit. It was dangerous to have unprotected sex. Wrong to be doing it in their place of employment.

Quite simply, any occasion that had involved physical contact between Alex and Layla had been...wild.

Snatched moments of time when nothing had mattered other than slaking a white-hot lust.

But this time it was different.

They had all the time in the world and that made them both oddly apprehensive about taking that next step. So, when Layla suggested they had dinner at the tapas bar where she'd gone with Chloe a while back, Alex agreed without hesitation. It was a reprieve from more than making a decision about where and when they would next be naked together. It was also a way of keeping this to themselves. If they went out together to O'Malley's, the grapevine at Angel's would have been buzzing with the news within hours.

Because this felt so different it seemed right to keep it private. This was their business. The unfinished kind, and whatever they were planning to do to see it through to its conclusion was not something anyone else needed to know about.

Except...wasn't this supposed to be about throwing fuel onto the smouldering physical attraction that had never died between them? All they needed for that was a room with a bed. A hotel or motel, preferably, so that things didn't intrude too far into their personal lives.

Why were they here, in a vibrant but softly lit bar, about to share food and drink and conversation instead of some nice, uncomplicated sex?

Alex sighed audibly. He really had no idea. It had seemed such a good idea at the time. A way to put a hard day's work behind him and catch his breath before facing this new turning point in his life.

'So...' He raised his glass of beer in a mock salute as Layla looked up from the menu she'd been studying. 'Here we are.'

'Mmm.' Layla's gaze slid away from his and she lifted her glass of wine to take a sip. 'We've come quite a long way to get here, haven't we?'

She wasn't talking about negotiating rush-hour New York traffic to get to the meatpacking district on the banks of the Hudson River. And it was an accurate statement. They had both taken very different routes through life to get to this point.

Funny that it felt like a huge circle all of a sudden.

'Head of Paediatrics in one of the country's most

prestigious children's hospitals.' Alex tilted his head to show his respect for Layla's achievements. 'Well done, you.'

'Head of Paediatric Neurosurgery in the same hospital,' Laya responded. 'I think being sought after as the person most likely to save a child's life tops my ability to boss people around and keep things running smoothly.'

The sound Alex made was dismissive. 'I'm just doing my job. The best way I know how.'

'Dayna wouldn't say that. Neither would I. I…um… didn't get the chance to congratulate you earlier. That surgery today was amazing to watch.'

'Thanks.'

'You didn't mind having an audience?' There was an unspoken question in Layla's eyes. She wasn't talking about an audience in general. She was asking him whether it had bothered him to have *her* in the gallery. Whether it had brought back memories of the last surgery of his that she'd witnessed. The disaster that had been Jamie Kirkpatrick's case.

The very idea of talking about that was enough to send a chill down his spine. He'd factored in the way his past with Layla was so inextricably linked to Jamie's case but he hadn't bargained on having to talk about it.

How stupid was that? Jamie had been part of their story right from the get-go. The reason they had met in the first place. And Layla pulling the plug on that relationship the night before Jamie's surgery might not have been the end of things if that surgery had gone well. Alex might well have tried to find out what had gone wrong. Tried to fix things between them. But it hadn't gone well. His world had shattered and the shards had driven him and Layla as far apart as it was possible to get.

But here they were again.

A huge mistake?

Quite possibly. Alex could almost hear Callie's voice in his ear.

*I told you so, mate. You should've listened.*

At least he could try and avoid the subject. It was easy to pretend he hadn't picked up on the subtext of Layla's casual query.

'I'm used to having an audience,' he said lightly. 'Might close the gallery for Tommy's surgery, though.'

Layla toyed with her glass. 'Have you set a date?'

'Not before next week at the earliest. There's a lot of preparation needed.' Like there had been before Jamie's complex surgery. Alex ruthlessly squashed the comparison.

'Let me know if there's anything I can do to help.'

His nod was offhand as he opened his menu. Alex didn't intend involving Layla. 'Food looks good,' he said a moment later. 'What are you going to have?'

'Maybe *costillas*.' Layla looked up with a smile. 'The barbecued mini-ribs. Messy but so tasty. And some *pimentos rellenos*.'

Alex raised an eyebrow. Her accent was perfect. Odd from someone with blonde hair and blue eyes and the face of a prom queen. She hadn't aged at all in the last five years. She could still be someone's high-school sweetheart. The girl next door, if next door happened to be some vast Texan ranch.

'They're peppers stuffed with rice,' Layla told him. 'Do you like shrimp? Try the *gambas a la plancha*.'

But Alex wasn't thinking about food any more.

'You never used to speak Spanish.' The statement came out almost as an accusation. 'I've been meaning to ask you about that ever since you stepped in to interpret for Ramona.'

The night that had shown him the depth of the connection he still felt with Layla. The connection that had blazed into that astonishing encounter in the decontamination shower. Hell…even the hint of a memory of that night made Alex wonder afresh why they'd come here at all instead of locating the nearest available bed. He had to suck in a slightly ragged breath and focus on what Layla was saying.

'I got a job in Miami.' She sounded offhand. 'There was a huge immigrant Spanish community and I got frustrated at not being able to communicate properly.'

'So you did something about it.' The lopsided smile Alex could feel tugging at his lips was tinged with a mix of admiration and…sadness? This was pure Layla, as much as the way she hurled herself into an emotional involvement with small patients. Show her a challenge and she grabbed it with both hands.

Like the way she'd approached him when she'd been merely a baby doctor, working different rotations to see what she might want to specialise in. He'd already made a name for himself so it must have taken guts for her to approach him. To tell him about Jamie Kirkpatrick and the radical new neurological procedure she'd read about that could possibly cure the toddler.

What had pulled him in so decisively back then?

This cute woman who'd had the courage not only to suggest the procedure but intelligent enough to have done her homework and to be able to discuss it at a level well above what he would have expected from her years and experience?

Or had it been something far less conscious? The appeal of someone who could care so much about a patient? A person who had a heart as big as her home state?

The echoes of that first meeting were disturbing. Alex needed to get his head back to the present. Back to at least a semi-professional space.

'Why Miami?'

He was expecting the conversation to move into the medical merits of a large city hospital and the workload and experience gained. But Layla looked at him in silence for a long moment and then dropped her gaze.

'It was as far away as I could get.'

'From L.A.?'

A brief nod. '*And* Texas.'

Had she gone alone, then? She certainly would have had the courage to do that. Suddenly it was important to Alex to know *when* she'd done it. How soon after their affair her marriage had ended. Whether he needed to shoulder some of the blame.

'How long did you spend in Miami?'

'A bit over five years. Until I came to Angel's.'

The same time frame that Alex had spent in his own self-imposed exile.

And the last person she'd slept with, other than him, had been her *husband*?

Oh...*hell*...

A waiter arrived with fresh drinks and a notepad to take their orders. Alex told Layla to order for both of them and then listened to her rattle off the Spanish names of dishes. She had a conversation with the waiter in Spanish that made them both laugh but Alex couldn't raise as much as a smile. He drank his beer and waited until the waiter had gone and the noise of the bar closed around them again to create an oddly private atmosphere.

'Was it our affair that ended your marriage?'

Layla's eyes widened. Then she shook her head. 'It was already dead in the water, Alex. The affair would never have happened if that hadn't been the case.'

He nodded slowly. She wasn't just saying that to absolve him of any guilt. He knew enough about Layla to know how focussed her passion for anything was. If she'd felt that passionate about a man, nobody would have been able to distract her.

How lucky would a man be, to have that kind of passionate commitment from Layla?

'I did think about trying again to make it work,' Layla continued quietly. 'When I talked to my mother about it, she told me to "stop being so ridiculous". That marriage is for life and if it wasn't working then that was only because I wasn't working hard enough at it.'

Alex snorted. 'So your parents had the perfect marriage, then?'

It was Layla's turn to snort. 'That's the thing. My parents' marriage was like my whole life growing up. It only had to *look* perfect. That was all that mattered. Daddy was the mayor of Swallow Creek. Everybody knew he cheated on Momma repeatedly but nothing was ever said. It's like the whole town was in some kind of movie and they all knew the part they had to play to get to the happy ending.'

Alex was appalled. 'And you? What was your part?'

'Oh, I just had to be the perfect daughter. The town's

"golden girl". To do well at school and be the captain of the cheerleading team and the high school prom queen.'

'So you *were* a prom queen?'

'Yeah… Why'd you ask?'

'Never mind. Go on.'

'Well, I married my high-school sweetheart, of course. No prizes for guessing that Luke happened to have been the prom king.'

'Sure sounds like a movie script.' Alex's comment was light but something like anger was building. How could anyone have tried to put Layla into a box and keep her contained?

She was far too unique for that. Too…*special.*

She laughed at his comment but there was no amusement in the sound.

'Yeah…but I lost my lines somewhere along the way. I got ambitions past being a stay-at-home mum and parading the mayor's cute grandbabies at every community event. I got a bee in my bonnet about being a paediatrician instead.'

Alex was watching her face. She'd had to fight for that ambition?

'Luke wasn't happy about it but I wasn't going to let anyone stop me. I even dragged poor Luke to L.A. with me and he was like a fish out of water. I couldn't blame him for being so angry. He was miserable. *He* knew his lines and what's more, he was happy to be a part of that damned movie.'

'Where is he now?'

Layla smiled. 'Back in Swallow Creek, of course. Married to another girl from our school. Sally. They've got two cute kids already. Another one on the way. Maybe even twins this time.'

The first dishes of their meal arrived. The sticky ribs came with bowls of water that had lemon slices floating in them because the ribs had to eaten with fingers and they lived up to their name in stickiness.

They were delicious and, for some time, they both ate with enormous enjoyment. For Alex, there was more than the taste to savour. Watching the enthusiastic way that Layla could eat. The expression of bliss on her face. The way she sucked the sauce off her fingers before she dipped them in the lemon-scented water.

Man…it was getting hot in here.

The heat wasn't just being generated from physical attraction. There was a warmth coming from something much deeper. Something else that was very different this time.

It was as if Alex was meeting Layla for the first time. This wasn't the doctor he'd worked with. Neither was she the lover whose touch had driven anything else from his consciousness.

This was the real Layla. The woman who'd been a little girl growing up in Swallow Creek. Who'd had parents and a boyfriend and a husband. Who'd had a script laid out for her life and who'd chosen to rebel.

Who'd become a woman he'd fallen head over heels in love with once upon a time.

Who'd crushed him unmercifully at the worst possible time.

Alex's appetite deserted him but Layla didn't seem to notice. He shook his head when she offered him the last rib and she was happy to pick it up herself.

He waited until she finished it.

'Can I ask you a question?'

'Shoot.' Layla rinsed her fingers and dried them on her napkin. She reached for her wineglass.

'What was it that made you so sure we were over?' Alex hadn't planned the question. The pressure had built so fast he couldn't seem to prevent the words escaping from his mouth. From his heart. 'And why did you have to pick the night before Jamie's surgery?'

Oh...God...

Layla's hand shook so much she had to put the wineglass back on the table. Just when she really, really needed a rather large swallow of that wine, too.

She hadn't seen this coming. Not this fast, anyway.

The arrival of more food gave her a brief reprieve but it was obvious by the way they picked at the dishes after the waiter had gone that neither of them were hungry any longer.

Layla's head was a mess but she only had herself to blame for being put on the spot like this after being so open about her childhood. Telling Alex stuff she'd never told anyone.

It was because this felt so different.

She and Alex knew each other physically as intimately as any two people could know each other but they'd never really got acquainted on any other level, had they?

Five years ago Alex had known that her marriage had been in trouble. How could he not when he'd overheard that horrible row with Luke that night when she'd abandoned her husband yet again to work late on the preparation for Jamie Kirkpatrick's surgery?

All she'd known about Alex had been that he was a sinfully handsome and incredibly talented young neurosurgeon who had been well on his way to becoming a leader in his field. Nothing had prepared her for the sizzling chemistry between them and, with her emotions at breaking point in the wake of that row, she had done the unthinkable and made the first move on Alex.

She had started that affair.

She had ended it.

It must have been a new and unpleasant experience for Alex Rodriguez on both counts but Layla had been confident that he would be able to dismiss the effects in no time given his established reputation that would have scared any sensible woman off.

She hadn't been surprised by the information that he'd gone straight into the arms of another woman when he'd stepped off the plane in Australia. Par for the course. That the fling had been over quickly was also no surprise. But there had been nobody since then?

That was...disturbing.

Even more disturbing given the intensity in that dark gaze when he'd voiced a question that had clearly been haunting him.

*What was it that made you so sure we were over?*

Layla had been open with Alex tonight because this situation felt so different. As though they were meeting each other on a new level. Not a professional one, as they had when they'd embarked on Jamie's case together.

Not a physical one either, as they'd had from the moment Layla had put her arms around Alex's neck, stood on tiptoe and touched her lips to his that very first time.

Could she stop now? Be less than honest with him?

No. Of course she couldn't. Not when the compul-

sion to stop being dishonest had been the real reason
her life had fallen apart back then.

Layla pushed her food aside. It took courage to look
up and meet Alex's brooding gaze.

'I was living a lie, Alex. I always had been so I
should have been good at it but I'd added a new layer
of deception into my life. I was a married woman and
I was having an affair. I felt guilty and I also felt kind
of sick about it because I was doing what my father
had done so often and I knew how wrong it was. How
hurtful.'

Alex said nothing but he was listening to every word.
He didn't take his eyes off Layla, even when she had to
drop her own gaze and focus on the table. Grains of rice
had spilled from the spicy peppers and she moved each
one back towards the platter with the tip of her finger,
aware of the heaviness of being watched so intently.
The expectation that she had more to say. And she did.

'The first time we…we were together,' Layla continued quietly, 'I knew there was no going back in my
life. I thought I had something to go forward towards
but then I wasn't so sure.'

'Why not?' The words had a bewildered edge.

'You shut yourself away, Alex. The closer we got to
the date of Jamie's surgery, the more closed off you got.
The case was the only thing that mattered. I was…just a
distraction that you needed to avoid. It got to the point
that I couldn't even see the man I had fallen for so hard.'

A swift upward glance in the wake of that revelation
showed her that Alex had closed his eyes. Retreated inwards again?

'So I was stuck in the middle,' Layla said sadly. 'I
couldn't go back to what I'd had because you'd shown

me what there could be and…and I didn't think there was anything to go forward towards any more.' Her voice wobbled just a tiny bit. 'It was a really lonely place to be. A really scary place.'

Layla had to close her own eyes for a heartbeat. To gather another dose of courage to answer that second question.

'The night before Jamie's surgery? I was there, in the same room as you, but it felt like we were on different planets. I couldn't believe how thoroughly I'd managed to mess up my life and…I got angry. With myself. With you. With everything in my life that had led me to that moment.'

Layla sighed. 'When I get angry, I have to do something about it. So I snapped and did what my heart told me I needed to do. I'm hot-headed, I know that. Impulsive. I know that, too. I let my heart rule my head too often and I know it's not professional. You don't have to tell me that I get too emotionally involved with patients. I know that as well.

'But it's part of who I am and…even if I didn't know it at the time, I made the decision to stop being part of that movie the moment I met you. I want to live my own life and I want things to be true on the inside, not just look like they're true from the outside.'

Oh…God…if she said anything else, she was going to start crying. She pushed back her chair.

'Excuse me,' she muttered. 'I need to…to powder my nose.'

She pushed her way through the crowd of people in the bar, making for the ladies room.

'What's the hurry, sweetheart?' A young man laughed. 'Let me buy you a drink.'

Layla didn't even see his face. Barely registered the invitation. There were only two people in this scene right now and she'd just laid herself completely bare in front of the other one.

This kind of nakedness made her feel far more vulnerable than any physical exposure could have done. What would Alex be thinking at the moment? Would he realise that she'd offered her heart on a plate back there? That, if he felt in any way inclined to exact revenge on the way she'd treated him, he now had the opportunity to carve her heart up into tiny pieces?

Layla needed a few minutes here. She was quite capable of gathering every ounce of courage she possessed and wrapping it around herself like a force-field. She'd already proved she was a survivor so she could survive whatever Alex had to say when she returned to their table.

She just needed a minute or two, that was all.

Alex watched Layla threading her way through the crowd. He saw some young jerk try to catch her attention and he knew that Layla hadn't even seen him.

He couldn't move a muscle. Couldn't even blink for the longest time. Talk about being walloped with an emotional sledgehammer.

If only he'd *known*.

Oh, he knew he'd pulled away from Layla. It hadn't been an easy thing to do but he'd done it because Jamie's surgery was going to make or break his career. Success had represented the future and the way he'd felt about Layla had had the potential to undermine everything he'd thought was rock solid in his life up until then.

That his career was all that mattered.

That emotional entanglements had to be avoided at all costs.

And maybe part of him had been aware that success had a new connotation. That the future had to be good enough for Layla to want to be a part of it. But had he told her why he was pulling away and erecting barriers?

No.

Why not?

Because that would have meant admitting how important she had been to him. That she'd had the potential to change his entire life if he could bring himself to trust her completely.

And he hadn't been able to.

He'd proved himself correct in withholding that trust because Layla had proved herself untrustworthy. She'd hurt him.

But he'd brought it on himself, hadn't he?

If only he'd known about what made her tick. About the way she'd been raised.

About that lonely place between turning points that had scared the hell out of her.

And most of all about the way she'd felt about him. What had she said? *The man she'd fallen so hard for?*

Alex could see Layla coming back towards the table now. Her chin was held high but the vulnerability in her body language was heart-breaking.

You could never turn the clock back. But Layla had been so honest with him. If nothing else, she deserved as much in return.

She sat down, eyed the leftover food and grimaced and then, slowly, raised her gaze to meet his.

Alex swallowed carefully. 'There was a bright spot, you know.'

Those bright blue eyes clouded with confusion. 'Sorry?'

'In the whole disaster that was Jamie's case and what happened after it…there *was* a bright spot.'

'Oh?'

'That's how Cade and I reconnected. He saw my mug shot in the papers, read about the malpractice suit and it was enough to make him ready to talk to me again for the first time in nearly a decade.'

He could see the stream of questions that Layla was dying to ask. It must have taken a real effort for her to remain silent.

'Any dysfunction in your family was hidden under a pretty exterior,' Alex said quietly. 'The problems with mine were there for everybody to see. There's probably a fat file buried somewhere with photographs of all the injuries I turned up to the emergency department with.'

'Oh, my God…' Layla breathed. 'From your *parents*?'

'Not my mother,' Alex said swiftly. 'No way. The only thing she ever did wrong was to marry an alcoholic bastard after my dad died. Cade's father.' He paused for a moment. 'No, maybe the worst thing she did was to get breast cancer and die.'

Layla's eyes had already widened with shock. Now they took on a brightness that suggested tears. Alex had to look away. He wasn't doing this to try and garner sympathy. He just wanted things to be equally honest between them.

'How old were you?'

'Ten. Cade was seven. He was safe enough, being Tony's son. I was the unwanted burden. A stepkid he'd never wanted in the first place. Anyway…' Alex wasn't going to dwell on those dark years of abuse. 'I upped and left when I was sixteen because I couldn't take it any more. Cade thought I'd abandoned him and he got pretty angry. By the time I tried to talk to him on his eighteenth birthday he didn't want anything more to do with me. I thought I'd lost my only living relative for ever but, thanks to the case, he made the first move.

'I'll always be grateful that he stood up to be counted when I needed it so much. He was about the only person who did. We've cleared up a lot of stuff since then and…well, I feel like I've got my brother back. So, that was a bright spot.'

Alex's smile was tight. There was no flicker of a response from Layla's lips.

'I'm sorry.' Her voice was choked. 'I felt so guilty… about everything. Luke, you…Jamie… I had no idea what to do about any of it and so I took the coward's way out and did nothing.'

'You didn't have anything to feel guilty about as far as Jamie was concerned. If I hadn't always had the ability to separate my personal stuff from my professional duties I would never have become a surgeon in the first place. What happened was a complication that none of us could have foreseen and, even if we had, we wouldn't have been able to do anything about it.'

'But it was me who persuaded you to try that new procedure in the first place. Because I'd fallen in love with Jamie and had got too involved and I was so determined to grab at any straw.'

'He would have died within weeks without the surgery. Technology has got a whole heap better now and I've perfected that technique since then as well. I'll probably use it for Tommy's operation.' Alex wanted to erase the frown lines creasing Layla's forehead. 'So, that's another bright spot, isn't it?'

Layla stared at him.

'What?'

'I can't believe you're trying to put a positive spin on any of this. You have every reason to hate me. I thought—'

'I don't hate you, Layla,' Alex cut in as she struggled to find words.

It was true. He didn't.

He couldn't have said exactly how he felt about her now other than an overwhelming physical attraction because the trust he'd been prepared to give her had been shattered and Alex had no idea whether it was even possible to repair something like that.

Maybe it was just as well he didn't need to say anything else just then. The waiter came back and eyed the plates of food on their table.

'You guys all done?'

'Yeah…' When Layla nodded to back him up, Alex pulled out his wallet and produced a credit card. 'We're all done here.'

Outside the bar, it was immediately apparent that the only completed business between them was the meal.

'Time to head home?' Alex asked.

Layla nodded.

'I don't live too far from here,' Alex heard himself saying. 'Come home with me?'

Layla hadn't expected that invitation. He could see the surprise in her eyes followed by a glow of…what? Pleasure? *Hope?*

He didn't want to try and analyse whatever it was because if he did, he might be tempted to run for cover.

What had happened to the idea of a hotel or motel and some nice, uncomplicated sex?

Alex had no idea. And when Layla's hand connected with his as they started walking, he laced his fingers through hers. When he felt the warmth of her hand and the responding pressure he was aware of a wash of relief that told him he was heading down the right track even if he had no idea of the destination.

Whatever was happening here had become about a lot more than simply sex.

Yes...things were very different.

# CHAPTER EIGHT

ALEX'S APARTMENT IN the midtown suburb was tiny. No more than a single, ground-level room in an old brownstone terraced complex but it was cleverly designed, with a kitchen tucked into a back corner and a comfortable living space featuring a huge couch and a widescreen television taking up two-thirds of the entire floor area. Bare wooden steps led up to a sleeping loft and beneath that was a closed-off bathroom and an open office that was clearly well used. The desk around the computer, like the coffee table in the living area, was strewn with papers and reference books festooned with sticky notes.

There was only one window but it was huge and above the heavy rectangle of the sash windows was a semicircle of coloured glass that gave the whole window the appearance of an archway. The original character of the historic building could also be seen in the richly polished floorboards and the rough whitewash covering the old brickwork of the interior walls.

Layla fell in love on the spot. When she came out of the compact bathroom a few minutes after her arrival she stood for a moment, soaking it all in. Alex hadn't turned on any lights but he hadn't drawn the curtains either and the streetlight gave everything a soft golden glow. Through the window she could see the wide steps that led into the building and the intricate wrought-iron fence that shut them off from the rest of the world.

Them?

Layla looked over her shoulder, expecting to see Alex in the kitchen.

He wasn't there and she caught her breath and held it, aware of spinning sensation that had nothing to do with how much wine she'd had to drink at the tapas bar.

'Up here.'

He'd only spoken softly but the small space seemed to catch Alex's voice and bounce it so it felt like his mouth was right against her ear.

'Waiting for you,' he added.

Oh…my… Layla kicked off her shoes and moved to the wooden stairs. *Stairway to heaven*, she thought, and almost snorted with laughter. Except that this didn't feel at all funny.

It didn't feel anything like it usually did when she knew she was on the verge of having sex with Alex either. Where was the heat that fried her brain and made her aware of nothing more than his scent? His taste? His *touch*…?

She climbed slowly and when she got to the top there was nowhere to go other than the bed.

And the bed was filled with Alex.

There was more than enough light to see the sheen of the olive-brown skin of his bare chest, the copper discs of his nipples amongst the scattering of dark hair that arrowed down to the crumpled duvet covering his legs. There was even enough light to see the question in his dark eyes. A sudden doubt. Was he suddenly as unsure about this as she was?

'Layla?'

She couldn't say anything. Couldn't even hold Alex's gaze because the heat wasn't there to fry her brain and it felt, ridiculously, like it was the first time they were making love and Layla was aware of an extraordinary sensation.

For maybe the first time in her life Layla was overcome by crippling shyness and she had no idea what to do about it. She felt completely lost for a moment. For as long as it took to raise her eyes and meet that dark gaze again.

For a long, long moment they held eye contact. And then Alex was moving. He knelt on the bed and held out his hands and Layla took them. He pulled her gently and her legs buckled and then she was kneeling on the bed too. Still holding her hands, Alex leaned in and kissed her lips. A soft touch. A wordless question.

Did she want this?

Oh…*yes*…

Layla's lips parted beneath Alex's and he took the invitation to deepen the kiss. With the first, exquisitely slow stroke of his tongue Layla knew that the heat was still there. It was all around them. Inside them. But, instead of an overwhelming conflagration, this time it was under control. They could play with it. Luxuriate in it. Take all the time they wanted and revel in every moment.

Still locked in that first kiss, Alex loosened Layla's top and they broke the kiss so that she could lift her arms while he pulled it off. And then his head dipped and she felt his lips on the side of her neck and she tipped her head back with a sigh as his kisses trailed down. He pushed the straps of her bra over her shoulders as his mouth reached the top of her breasts and then he kissed her lips again as he unfastened her bra. A one-handed movement that advertised a skill he might not have practised for a while but which he certainly hadn't lost.

Still kneeling on the bed together, Layla pressed her bare breasts against his chest and felt Alex's hand slip beneath her waistband to cup her buttocks and draw her even closer.

Oh, yeah...the heat was there all right. Layla could feel herself slipping, deliciously slowly, into the mindless pleasure that only Alex had ever been able to give her. Her fingers skimmed over the hard planes of muscle on his back, over the soft skin on the sides of his neck and then they buried themselves in the soft silk of his hair.

Alex's hands mirrored hers. She could feel a trail of fire from each of the fingers on his hands as they covered her back, his palms dipping into the curve above her hipbones. Touching her ribs and then that sensitive skin beneath her breasts on their way up. His hands became completely lost in the tumble of her hair and Layla could actually feel the ends of her pale hair tangling with the dark hair on Alex's arms.

She'd never known that touch could be like this. That every cell in her body could be *this* connected. *This* sensitive. She breathed in the air that Alex was breathing out and it seemed to have more oxygen in it. She could taste the spice of Spanish food in his mouth. Or was that just the taste of Alex himself?

The kiss went on. And on. Until Layla felt herself

being gently lowered onto the bed and Alex began peeling the rest of her clothing from her body. The process seemed unbearably slow and she tried to help but Alex caught her hands.

'I want to do this,' he murmured, and she could hear the smile in his voice. 'It's like Christmas.'

Unwrapping a gift?

He saw her body as a *gift*?

Oh… Layla couldn't have moved to help him now. Her head sank back into the pillow and she closed her eyes as a wave of an emotion she couldn't identify swept her away.

She had known how good it was to be touched by Alex. To touch him. Her body had never forgotten the ecstasy of ultimate closeness. But it had always had an edge of something frantic to it. An insane race to capture satisfaction before they could be discovered. Before something, or someone, in the outside world intervened and ripped them apart. It had never been like this.

Layla had never imagined someone honouring her body like this. Worshipping her with the touch of his hands. The tips of his fingers. The silky glide of his tongue. She wanted to do the same for him. To explore his whole body. Slowly. To touch and taste every inch of his skin. To elicit sounds from him like the tiny whimper of need she heard coming from her own throat.

But not yet. She couldn't wait that long. Alex might still have control over that burning desire but she was rapidly losing hers. She was on familiar ground now. Wanting Alex so much that she felt she might die if it didn't happen. Now.

'Alex…please…' She writhed under the unbearably

gentle onslaught of his lips and tongue as they touched the core of her being. 'I need you. Inside me. *Now...*'

He responded with the swiftness of a whip cracking. A few seconds' delay as he wrenched open the bedside cabinet and then ripped into a foil package and then he was there. Between her legs. Looking down at her and touching her face with his gaze as intensely as the hard heat she could feel touching the entrance to the place she desperately wanted him to fill.

Layla was drowning in his eyes. She reached up to pull him closer and couldn't recognise her own voice as she cried out his name.

Layla woke first, a little before dawn, knowing that she'd had nowhere near enough sleep to face a day at work, but she didn't care. The need to go downstairs to the bathroom had woken her but she let herself drift into consciousness without moving a muscle.

She let herself become aware of everything she could feel. The heavy weight of Alex's leg draped over one of hers. The ridge of his arm beneath her head. The rise and fall of his chest against her cheek. The heavy grunt of his breathing that was almost a snore because he was still so deeply asleep.

Layla hadn't intended staying here all night. She must have fallen asleep first, because if Alex had she would remember it. She would have agonised over whether to wake him up to tell him she was going or just slip away and leave him a note or something.

Shifting her head carefully so as not to wake him, Layla moved so that she could see his face. His lips were parted slightly. Long, dark lashes nestled on his cheeks.

She had never seen Alex asleep before. He looked so peaceful.

So young.

Something huge squeezed in her chest as she remembered their conversation of the night before and put the pieces of the puzzle together. She knew now what Cade had meant when he'd said that Alex knew too much. That he was too quick to jump to conclusions about a small patient who might have been abused. She could understand why Alex had been so angry. So ready to deliver a brutal blow to Ramona's boyfriend.

It broke her heart to think of any child being abused. But to know that *Alex* had been injured so badly, physically and emotionally, went beyond heart-breaking.

Tears stung Layla's eyes. She wanted to wrap her arms around him and hold him to her heart. She couldn't fix the past but she could protect him now.

She could let him know that he hadn't deserved a childhood like that. That he should have been treasured and loved. She had to move more now. So that she could lift her hand and touch his face. Just with a single fingertip. A butterfly's kiss on his temple. To let him know that he was loveable. That he *was* loved.

By her.

Oh…God…

Those tangled, dark lashes flickered and Alex's eyes opened at the same instant that the realisation hit Layla that this wasn't only about physical attraction. And it never had been. Not for her.

So much for throwing fuel onto the ashes of a smouldering lust to let it burn itself out. What Layla was feeling now was burning so brightly that she knew it would never go out. She never had, and never could, love anybody other than Alex like this.

Maybe it was just as well it took as long as it did for Alex to surface completely. That he reached for her while he was still more than half-asleep and that their slow kiss reignited their earlier passion. He would never know how tenderly Layla had touched him. Or see the tears that had filled her eyes.

Talk about mind-blowing.

Alex had often wondered what it would have been like to have the luxury of spending a whole night with Layla.

Now he knew.

Had he really thought that a sleazy motel room would have been a good idea?

Or that the sex would have been satisfying but uncomplicated?

Layla was in the shower now. Alex had pulled jeans on but nothing else and he was making a pot of coffee while he waited for his turn to freshen up. He'd been invited to share the shower. Nobody could have missed the flash of disappointment—confusion, even—at his swift turning down of the offer.

God knew, he'd *wanted* to share that shower.

So why wasn't he in there? Soaping Layla's gorgeous body. Wrapping her in a towel and pulling her into a kiss as steamy as the bathroom, while they were both wet and slippery and smelling like the soap?

Because it would have been a step too far, that's why.

And last night hadn't been? Alex shook his head, emitting an incredulous huff as he spooned ground coffee into the jug.

It wasn't supposed to have been like that.

So...*tender.*

It had never been like that before so he hadn't expected it. Hadn't expected to feel like that. As though he wanted to make it up to Layla for having had to live a lie for most of her life.

To show her that *he* was real. That *this* was real.

And it wasn't, was it?

What was eating at his gut right now was the knowledge that they hadn't been having sex for half the night. They'd been making love.

And that was a kind of lie all on its own because if you made love like that you were making some kind of promise about the future, weren't you?

And he couldn't make that kind of promise to anyone. Especially not Layla. She'd proved she could turn her back and walk off if it suited her.

The kettle boiled and he poured the water over the coffee grounds. The smell hit him and he breathed in deeply as he fitted the plunger. Time to wake up, Rodriguez, he almost snarled inwardly. Don't even think of going there.

*Trust nobody. Except yourself.*

It was the only way to stay safe.

The rap on his door was unexpected. Alex crossed the room and opened it to find Cade, who held up a large paper bag.

'Breakfast, man.' Cade was grinning. 'I've got news.' He entered the apartment with the ease of someone who knew they were welcome. 'Mmm. You've got coffee ready. Perfect timing.'

They both knew that the clunking sound advertised the shower being turned off. Cade was over by

the kitchen bench now, depositing the bag. His head
turned swiftly. He took in the fact that Alex was only
wearing jeans and that the button was still unfastened.
Then he turned to stare at the bathroom door.

'Oops. Sorry. Am I interrupting something?'

Alex shrugged, turning to push the door closed. He
didn't see the bathroom door opening.

'Nothing important,' he said lightly. 'I got lucky last
night, that's all.'

The shock of seeing Alex's half-brother standing directly in front of Layla as she came out of the bathroom
was nothing compared to hearing the dismissive words
that had just been spoken.

'Hey, Layla…' Cade looked embarrassed. On her behalf, perhaps, after hearing that she'd just been a play-
mate for the night? 'I should…um…head off and get to
work or something.'

'Nah…stay and have some breakfast, now you're
here.' Was that relief in Alex's tone? An escape route
from the intimacy of sharing a meal after the night
they'd had? 'Layla doesn't mind, do you, Layla?'

'Not at all. I'll just throw some clothes on.'

'And I'll jump into the shower. I'll only be two minutes.'

Layla dressed as quickly as she could. She was planning on skipping breakfast. Alex had company and, besides, she needed to get home and changed so she didn't
turn up at Angel's wearing the same clothes she'd left
in yesterday.

But Alex was coming out of the bathroom as she
went back down the stairs. He had a towel knotted

around his hips and an apology written across his features.

What was he sorry for? That they'd been busted or because he'd dismissed what had happened between them last night as 'nothing important'?

He watched her pick up her handbag and stepped closer.

'Don't go,' he said softly. 'Please? At least have a coffee?'

This was confusing. Maybe the intention of last night had simply been to indulge the physical attraction they shared in the hope that it would burn itself out, but they both knew that it had been bigger than simply sex. That something had changed.

That they hadn't picked up where they'd left off years ago.

They'd made a fresh start.

And this time it actually held the potential of going somewhere.

If they let it. If they wanted it to.

Layla felt a wash of that emotion she'd experienced watching Alex sleep. She knew how damaged this beautiful man had to be, whether he was aware of it or not. Did she really expect him to trust her straight off? To trust that what had happened last night was real?

Maybe she could take the first step. She could let him know that she wasn't about to run away if things got tough. That, this time, she was quite prepared to do whatever it might take to be with him.

She smiled at him. 'Coffee would be great. And some of whatever's in that bag, if there's enough, because it smells divine and I'm hungry enough to eat a horse.'

'Is that what they do in Texas?' Cade welcomed her into the kitchen with a grin. 'Eat horse for breakfast?'

'Only if there aren't any griddle cakes and black-eyed peas.' Layla eyed the bag he was ripping open. 'Bagels. Yum.'

'Help yourself.' Cade watched as Layla swiped a smear of cream cheese from the bag and licked it off her finger. 'You and Alex, huh? And there I was, telling people that those rumours were rubbish.'

Alex had dressed himself with impressive speed. He was buttoning his shirt as he joined them but he paused to drape his arm over Layla's shoulder.

'Layla and I go way back,' he told Cade. 'Pre-Brisbane days.'

'Ahh…' Cade looked as though he was retrieving some more of those rumours. The ones about Layla being married at the time, perhaps. Or maybe he was putting two and two together about the unpleasant legal repercussions of Jamie's disastrous surgery and coming up with a reason for them splitting up that nobody would want to talk about. He gave his head a tiny shake and cleared his throat.

'Speaking of Brisbane,' he said to Alex, 'I was busy myself last night. Having a long conversation with your friend Callie.'

Layla was trying not to watch as Alex tucked his shirt into his pants and did up his fly and belt buckle. There was something about the inflection on the word 'friend' that sent a shaft of something nasty through her belly. Was Callie the one that Alex had had the fling with when he'd arrived on that side of the world?

Jealousy. That's what that nasty sensation was. Layla

had no right to feel this possessive. Good grief...what was happening to her here?

'She's talked me into taking the job,' Cade continued. 'I'm heading off as soon as I can work out my notice. Couple of weeks, tops.'

'Wow...you don't muck around.' Leaving his top buttons undone and his tie hanging loose, Alex filled a mug with coffee and took a big swallow. 'You sure you want to do this?'

'I'm not a kid any more, Alex. I get to make my own choices and learn from them if they turn out to be mistakes.' His gaze flicked to Layla and then back to his brother.

Layla caught her breath. Was Cade actually saying that he thought Alex having anything to do with her was a big mistake?

No. The sudden tension between the brothers suggested that some button had been pushed that had nothing to do with her. There were probably all sorts of triggers buried in their shared, stormy backgrounds. A background that Layla needed to take into consideration for all sorts of things. Like being patient with Alex if it took him a long time to trust her. And understanding his passionate reaction to cases of child abuse. Accepting his need for his own space at times to focus completely on the career that had been his way forward from a horrible start to his adult life.

The comment led to an awkward silence that Layla felt compelled to break.

'I should get going,' she said. 'I've got a big meeting at nine a.m. We're trying to find sponsors to help with the fundraising to update our MRI machine and it's a biggie. We were supposed to do it yesterday but the meeting got derailed when I had to see someone in Emergency.'

'I thought that was already sorted,' Cade said.

'What?'

'The social committee put out a flyer last week. They're hoping everyone will attend the big Halloween party they've got planned. That's down as a fund-raiser for the MRI.'

'Oh...I hadn't caught up with that.' Layla smiled at Cade. 'Thanks for the heads-up. It might help to encourage the sponsors. Any money from a hospital fundraiser will be great but we'll still need more. New technology doesn't come cheap.'

'It should raise heaps. Tickets are a hundred dollars and everyone's being asked to bring as many people as they can. It'll be Angel's staff and all the friends and relatives they can bring with them. The venue could hold a thousand people apparently.'

Layla blinked. That was some fundraiser. Why hadn't she heard about it already?

'You'll have to come,' Cade continued. He sent a crooked smile in Alex's direction and it looked like it was intended to be an olive branch. 'I'm heading out to a costume-hire place with a few others after work today. Want me to pick something out for you?'

'I don't do dress-ups.' The words were curt. And he was looking at Layla rather than Cade.

*I'm not going to pretend to be someone I'm not*, the silent message said.

Was he trying to tell her that he was real? That this—whatever was happening between them—was also real? On the inside as well as the outside?

'Neither do I,' Layla said, still holding Alex's gaze.

Then she looked at Cade and smiled. 'I'll be happy to buy a ticket, though.'

Cade shrugged. 'Well, if it turns out to be my farewell gig from Angel's, you'll have to come, costume or not.' His glance slid from Alex to Layla and back again and a corner of his mouth lifted. '*Both* of you.'

Was he giving his blessing to the idea of them as a couple now? Encouraging Alex?

This was doing her head in. It didn't matter where she stood with Cade but how Alex felt right now was very, very important. Did he still see this reunion as a means of putting out an old flame so that they could both move on and be able to work together without it creating any personal tension?

Had it really been her suggestion?

Yes. But she'd known, deep down, that there was more than just a flicker of hope that it could be more than that.

What had she done? She'd learned so much more about Alex, that's what. She'd stirred the ashes and discovered that she'd been in love with him right from the get-go and she'd only fallen deeper last night.

Had she set herself up for a devastating blow?

The thought was terrifying but there was nothing she could do about it. As far as she was concerned, the step they had taken now was irrevocable. It was Alex's call how it was going to play out because there was no way she could pull the plug on this.

Vulnerability was dangerous. It made you weak. Layla had learned very early in life that if you felt threatened you had to make yourself stronger. Take charge. Fake it till you made it and all that.

She lifted her chin. 'I really do have to go. Got a hospital to run. I'll see you boys later.'

At least with Cade there, the awkwardness of what to say or do in farewell was gone. There would be no lingering kiss. No promises of when they could be together again.

It was a good thing, Layla told herself firmly as she flagged down a taxi outside Alex's apartment.

A promise was only words and a promise could be broken.

Like hearts could?

# CHAPTER NINE

I T WAS AMAZING how quickly you could get used to a new routine. How quickly you could become lulled into a false sense of security. Within days, almost, Alex and Layla both stopped worrying about the rumours that might be circulating through Angel's. Now they didn't even bother to try hiding the fact that they were arriving for work together.

Tyler Donaldson wasn't about to let a chance slide by when he saw them standing near the huge fish tank in Angel's lobby one morning.

'You guys look as happy as pigs in muck,' he announced. His grin widened. 'Life's good, huh?'

'Hey, Ty.' Layla seemed happy to greet her old friend but Alex had spotted another early arrival at the hospital.

'Jack! Hey…haven't seen you for ages.'

'Alex…'

The handshake between the two men instantly morphed into a typically male, one-armed hug that involved a bit of back thumping.

Jack Carter held his hand out to Tyler. 'I haven't had a chance to congratulate you on fatherhood. How's it going?'

'I'm lovin' every minute of it.' Tyler shook Jack's hand but raised an eyebrow at the same time. 'And didn't I hear a rumour that you're gonna join the sleepless nights and nappy brigade? How's Nina doing?'

'Glowing,' Jack said proudly. 'Nearly five months along now.'

'She certainly is glowing,' Layla put in. 'I only caught up on that news myself last week. You must be thrilled, Jack.'

'Oh…for sure.'

'She told me that you'd adopted Janey and Blake, too.'

Jack shook his head. 'I know. Single man one minute, father of three the next. Life's full of amazing surprises, isn't it?'

'Mmm…' Alex caught just the flicker of a glance in his direction. 'I wouldn't disagree with that.'

He made no attempt to join in the conversation, however, because he had the uncomfortable sensation that he had been left alone in a parallel universe here. He wasn't disinterested because Jack Carter was his oldest friend. They'd been through medical school together. It had been Jack who'd set up this job for him at Angel's. They hadn't seen so much of each other since Jack had left to take up a full-time position at the pro bono centre in Harlem. He'd been Jack's best man at the wedding, of course, but that had been a long time ago now. Jack still did the odd consult here at Angel's and Nina was still a social worker but their paths didn't cross often enough. Perhaps that was why he hadn't noticed Nina's shape changing. Not that he wasn't happy for Jack because Jack looked on top of the world.

He just couldn't imagine it for himself. In the wake

of his childhood—and Cade's—the responsibility of bringing a child into the world was not something he would touch with the proverbial bargepole.

Layla seemed to be more than happy to be discussing the expected arrival date and how Nina's younger siblings were feeling about the addition to the new family. There was something about the animation in her face that rang a warning bell for Alex.

Layla would want children.

The conviction came from nowhere and it felt curiously...disturbing. She may not have wanted to settle down and produce grandbabies for the mayor of Swallow Creek to show off but...hell...she *loved* kids. Given the way she got so involved with her small patients, Alex could imagine how fiercely she would love her own children. And she'd be an amazing mother.

Why was the thought so disturbing?

Because it would have to be another man who would be the father of those children?

He should be fine with that. This new...fling with Layla was not going to be permanent. They were just burning off a lingering physical attraction and he had absolutely no desire for it to become anything more than that.

It *couldn't* because that would mean trusting Layla to the same extent he had mistakenly trusted her the first time round. And she'd betrayed that trust and left him to fall into such a dark place that he was determined he would never go anywhere near there again.

What the hell had he been thinking, playing with fire like this again?

Totally unintended factors were sneaking into the

equation. Like the need to be with Layla as often as possible.

Like a flash of downright envy for the man who would be the father of her children.

Alex tuned back into the conversation between in time to hear Tyler excusing himself. Jack made an apologetic face as the big Texan doctor walked off with a wave.

'Sorry about that. Kids aren't really your thing, are they, Alex?'

Alex snorted, ignoring the odd glance that came his way from Layla. 'No. That's why I became a paediatric neurosurgeon. Speaking of which, I'm due at a ward round upstairs right about now. Maybe we can grab a beer at O'Malley's later?'

'Sounds good. But you don't get rid of me that easily. I'm heading upstairs myself.'

'Me too.' Layla stayed with them. 'How's it going at the centre, Jack?'

'It's great. I feel like I'm making a real difference.'

'I wouldn't mind getting involved myself. Would you have any use for a doctor who can speak Spanish?'

'Are you kidding? We'd snap up any free time you had.' Jack shot Alex a sideways glance. 'From what I hear, though, free time might be a bit thin on the ground.'

The reference to time prompted Layla to check her watch. 'Oh, help…I'm going to be late for that meeting.' She waved and someone moved to stop the elevator doors closing.

The elevator looked pretty full. 'I'm going to take the stairs,' Alex said. 'I'll catch you both later.'

'I'll join you.' Jack hung back as Layla raced off. 'I could do with the exercise.'

'You here on a consult?' Alex asked as they entered the stairwell.

'Not exactly. Nina's hoping to get a bit of free time so we can go visiting. She tells me that Tommy Jenner is on the ward.'

'Yep.' Alex didn't slow his stride as they climbed the first flights of stairs.

'And you're going ahead with the surgery?'

'Yep. Scheduled for Friday. We had to put it off because he picked up a bit of a bug last week.'

'I hope it goes well,' Jack said quietly. 'Nina's going to be holding her breath.'

'I might be, too.' Alex could feel his breathing now after three flights of stairs. He paused to take a quick glance through the window. You could see the end of the ambulance bay from here. And the line of rubbish skips. The basketball court was deserted. Maybe he could find Cade later and he could get a workout in. And maybe that would dispel this odd edginess that was building in the wake of those disturbing thoughts he'd just had about Layla's future family. No. Now that he thought about it, that edginess had had been building ever since that night with Layla.

That *first* night with Layla. They'd clocked up a few more since then.

And whatever it was between them didn't seem to be burning itself out. If anything, those flames were burning higher. Brighter. He'd issued the warning himself, hadn't he? If you played with fire, things could get out of hand. Somebody could get badly hurt.

Had he been so confident of his ability to stay detached that he'd assumed the person who got hurt wouldn't be him?

'It was your first day at Angel's, wasn't it?' Jack was looking out the window beside him. 'When you got caught up in Tommy's case?'

'Yeah… It was a memorable elevator ride with Nina in there, trying to calm Mike down when he was furious with people trying to take Tommy away for treatment.'

'Hardly surprising when you look back on it all. There he was, struggling to be a single dad to a kid who'd been so traumatised by being left in a house with his dead mother for days and everybody assumed he was abusing Tommy. It's no wonder he went off the edge but it did make it harder to see what was really going on.'

'Not for Nina.'

'No… But she's a woman in her own class of amazing.' Jack's smile held a tenderness that made Alex feel left out again. 'She loves Tommy to bits. She's taught me a thing or two about taking notice of more than the clinical picture we get from patients.'

'Hmm.' Alex watched an ambulance turning into the bay. Layla did that. Was it a female thing?

Or maybe Layla was in her own class of amazing, too.

'She's really excited about the prospect of him getting a new mother soon. Is it true that Mike got involved with one of the oncology nurses?'

'Yeah…Gina. She's lovely. He's planning to propose if the surgery goes well.'

Jack sucked in a breath. 'No pressure, then…?'

Alex grunted and turned away from the window.

He was more than ready to tackle a few more flights of stairs. Jack was half a step behind him.

'So...how's it working out?'

'With Tommy? We'll have to wait and see.'

'No...I meant at Angel's. That first day was a while back now and I haven't been around for months. You happy here?'

'Yep.' Until Layla had arrived anyway. And now that they'd found a way to deal with the tension, Alex had to admit he was feeling happier than he had in a long time.

Years. More than five years, to be exact.

They climbed the rest of the way in silence but paused again after Alex had pushed open the fire-stop doors on the eighth floor.

'I heard about the Kirkpatrick case hitting the grapevine,' Jack said. 'How on earth did that happen? I was quite confident that it was going to be buried.'

'Cade didn't realise it was being kept quiet.'

'Oh...' Jack's glance conveyed his understanding of the turbulent relationship the brothers had had. 'Problem?'

'Could have been,' Alex admitted. 'In the end it turned out to be a good thing. Gave us the chance to resolve a few issues that needed airing. Our relationship is better than it's ever been now.'

Jack's nod was pleased. 'That's great.'

'Yes and no.'

'Why no?'

'He's planning to take off. Follow my footsteps and go for a new job in Australia. In my old hospital, no less.' Alex rubbed his forehead. 'I've only got myself to blame. I told him that an old friend there was on the hunt for a prenatal surgeon.'

They could have left the conversation there and gone their separate ways. Jack was here to visit Tommy and Alex was going to be late to start his ward round but that edginess was suddenly boiling to the surface. Alex stayed where he was, with the safety of the wall right behind him.

'Do you ever get the feeling that life goes in circles, Jack?'

If Jack was disconcerted by the subtext, he didn't show it. Like the good friend he was, he simply moved a bit closer, giving the impression that he had all the time in the world to talk. Two men having a bit of a yarn. Or two doctors having a quiet word about a patient.

'Circles?' he prompted gently.

'Yeah. I had Cade in my life and then out of it for too many years. Back in it again when he saw the publicity about the Kirkpatrick case and then out of it when I took off to Australia. Now he's back but he's planning to take off himself.'

'You won't lose touch. Email's great. Phone calls by computer even better. There's nothing to stop you taking a holiday either. I'll bet you miss all the sun and those fabulous beaches.'

But Alex wasn't finished. 'It's the same with my job. Has it occurred to you that Tommy's case is horribly similar to Jamie Kirkpatrick's? That I'm back where I was all those years ago, about to tackle a surgery that could go belly up and wreck more than one life?'

'It's a tough call.' Jack's face was creased with sympathy. 'But you can't think about it like that. Be proud that you are one of the few people that can offer any hope at all in a case like this. Mike's not going to sue you if it doesn't go well. From what Nina's told me, he's well aware of the risks. He's incredibly grateful that you're even prepared to try.'

Alex shook his head. 'I'm not sure I should be. I'm not sure I could live with myself if it doesn't go well.'

'If you don't try, he'll die,' Jack said bluntly. 'Could you live with that?'

Alex sighed. He started to rub his forehead again but, instead, ran stiff fingers through his hair. 'It's not just those circles,' he admitted quietly. 'There's also…'

No. He couldn't say her name. Talking about it might mean he'd hear something he really didn't want to hear. He might have to admit what was really going on deep in his own heart.

He didn't have to say her name. Jack's gaze held a sympathetic understanding.

'Layla?'

That heat at the sound of her name was anger. Something very private was being exposed. Something Alex had been avoiding looking at too closely himself until this morning. 'How the hell did you find out about that?'

Jack's smile was conciliatory. 'You forget that I'm still involved with Angel's. That Nina still works here. We…ah…hear things.'

'Like what?' Oh, God…had the grapevine somehow got information about what had happened in the decontamination shower that night?

'Just that there's a certain vibe whenever you two are in the same room. A rumour that someone saw a stolen kiss somewhere. I wasn't sure I believed it until I saw you two together this morning. You may as well have a neon sign above your heads.'

'Oh…' Alex couldn't deny that vibe. It felt like the very air came alive with sparks whenever he was within

sight of Layla. Hardly surprising that other people could
feel the heat. Had he really been bothered a few weeks
back that Layla was stalking him and that their paths
seem to cross far too often? It couldn't be often enough
now. He really was in trouble here, wasn't he?

'There you are...' The voice came from the nearby
elevator as the doors slid open. 'I've been looking for
you, Jack.' Nina came towards them, smiling.

Alex found himself staring at the elevator as the
doors slid shut again. Stupid to be disappointed that
Layla wasn't amongst the people left. Her elevator
would have delivered her to the top floor long ago.
About when he'd been staring out the window, thinking about shooting hoops.

'Hi, babe.' If Jack had looked happy discussing his
impending fatherhood, it was nothing compared to the
joy on his face now. 'How's it going?'

'Wonderful. I've got our tickets for the Halloween
ball.' Nina laughed. 'The suggestion was made that I
could go as a pumpkin and all I would need is an orange
dress.' She patted her belly. 'What do you think, Alex?'

'I think you could go as something far more glam-
orous than a pumpkin.'

Nina was still grinning. 'A witch, maybe?' She
pointed at Jack. 'Don't you dare say a word.'

Jack managed to look totally innocent and highly
amused at the same time. He cleared his throat. 'You
going to the ball, Alex?'

'Nah...though it looks like it's going to be Cade's
farewell and he's got some idea of us going in match-
ing costumes.'

'The Brothers Grimm?' Nina had clearly caught

the excitement that seemed to be taking over Angel's. 'Tweedledee and Tweedledum?'

Jack shook his head. 'Come on. Time to take you away. Let's go and see if Tommy's up for a visit.'

'I'll catch you later.' Alex could see Ryan O'Doherty coming through the ward doors. Looking for his senior colleague, no doubt, in order to get the ward round under way.

'We'll grab that beer.' Jack raised an eyebrow and his smile was encouraging. 'And you know what?'

'What?'

'Circles can be good. Sometimes they can take you back to a place you didn't know you wanted to be.'

Tommy Jenner was getting a lot of visitors today.

Mike was there, of course. He had taken time off work to be with his son for the duration of this hospital admission. Gina was rostered on as Tommy's nurse whenever she was on shift in the ward but she had other patients to attend to as well. Jack and Nina had been in this morning and Tommy's surgeons, Alex and Ryan, were checking up on their young patient at frequent intervals. As chief paediatrician, it was only to be expected that Layla was taking a special interest in this case as well.

The irony that the medical problem Tommy was facing was so similar to the one Jamie Kirkpatrick had faced and that this surgery was happening when she and Alex were in the fragile new stages of another relationship was lying more heavily in the back of Layla's mind every day, but it still seemed like a bonus to find Alex in Tommy's room when she made her own visit in the afternoon.

It was always a bonus when their paths crossed during working hours these days. Layla could see him in the room before she tapped lightly on the door and pushed it open so she hesitated for a heartbeat, just to enjoy the moment.

It was kind of like when you were a kid and you'd been given the most amazing Christmas or birthday gift, she decided. It wasn't that you necessarily wanted to play with it all the time but it was very important to keep it somewhere where you could see it as often as possible.

So you knew it was real.

The reality of this new connection with Alex could be found in the most fleeting glance or the hint of a smile. During a professional conversation that had a subtext only the two of them were aware of. It was delicious.

Addictive.

So much so that Layla knew the instant it changed and that happened the second she walked into Tommy's room. Alex raised his gaze from the notes he was reading to nod and smile an acknowledgment of her presence and the smile was the same as always, but Layla still knew.

It was the abrupt way the eye contact had ended. A split second in time, maybe, but it was enough to let Layla know it was happening again.

Alex was pulling away.

'Hey, Tommy.' Layla smiled at both Tommy and his dad. 'How're y'all doing?'

'Me an' Dad are having haircuts tomorrow. We're getting it *all* shaved off.'

'Wow.' Layla hitched a hip on the end of the bed.

Close to where Alex was standing, flipping pages on the chart, but he didn't look up. Was it her imagination or did he shift just a little further away? 'Both of you, huh?'

'Yeah...' Mike ran a hand through his own hair and then ruffled his son's. 'We're going to have a race to see who can grow hair the fastest after Tommy has his operation.'

Layla was quite confident she was the only person here who was aware of the tension emanating from Alex. Or that it had just increased a notch. Tommy would have to survive his surgery if his hair was going to grow back.

'I asked Gina if she wanted to shave her hair off too,' Tommy told her. 'But she said she didn't *really* want to.'

Layla laughed. 'I'm not surprised. It's a bit different for girls.'

'Why?'

'I guess we're not as brave as boys. And we like our hair too much.'

'Dad said he likes Gina's hair just the way it is. She's got pretty hair, so I guess it's OK if she doesn't do the race.'

Alex was scribbling something onto the chart and even his writing sounded tense. Layla could hear the scratching and tapping against the clipboard holding the papers. She wished she'd never told Alex about Mike's plan to ask Gina to marry him if the surgery went well.

Of course he was pulling away. The pressure was building and he needed to focus. It wouldn't be like the last time this had happened because this time she understood. She could give him space if that's what he needed. She was older and wiser now and she wasn't

going to have a hissy fit because she felt she wasn't getting enough attention.

She was starting to feel a bit tense about it all herself,
in fact. It was kind of unfair that life was throwing a
testing time like this at them so fast. They needed more
time to build trust. They were making a fresh start and
it had a promise that was precious.

She had way too much to lose if things went wrong.

Could Alex feel the reassurance she was trying to
project? If he did, he didn't acknowledge it. When he
finally looked up from the chart, he looked straight at
Tommy.

'There's another doctor who's going to come and visit
you tomorrow, buddy. Dr Jill. She's an anaesthetist. Do
you know what that is?'

'No. What?'

'She's the one who's in charge of helping you go to
sleep so you can have your operation. It's called having an anaesthetic.'

Tommy's bottom lip wobbled. 'But I'll wake up
again, won't I?'

'You won't even know you've been asleep,' Alex
promised. 'You'll close your eyes and then it'll feel
like you just open them again straight away but it'll
all be over.'

'Will my head hurt?'

'We'll give you medicine to stop it hurting.'

'Will I have a big bandage?'

'You sure will. And you'll be in a special place called
Intensive Care for a few days.'

Layla could see the way Mike's throat moved as he
swallowed hard.

'I'll be there, too,' he told Tommy, leaning down

to give him a kiss. 'I'll be right beside you when you wake up.'

The tiny break in Mike's voice almost undid Layla and she could see a tiny muscle jumping in Alex's jaw. She forced herself to sound bright.

'You know what's going to happen next week?' she asked Tommy. 'What you've got to look forward to when you come back to the ward?'

'No.' Tommy was frowning deeply, as though trying to figure out how to respond to the charged atmosphere around him. 'What?'

'It's going to be Halloween. There'll be lots of decorations and some of the doctors and nurses put on silly costumes and have a parade. And there'll be all sorts of yummy treats for everybody to eat.'

'What sort of treats?'

'Candy,' Layla said confidently. 'And ice cream and…and…*spiders*.'

Tommy's jaw dropped. Then he giggled.

'I'll leave you to it,' Alex said, moving towards the door. 'I'll see you tomorrow, Tommy.'

Layla watched him leave.

And she had the horrible feeling that she was watching him walk away from *her*.

Which was ridiculous. Wasn't it?

They were in a better place than they'd ever been.

And she was going to do whatever it took to keep them there.

# CHAPTER TEN

THERE WAS COMFORT to be found in a case that required going the extra mile.

It was a lesson Alex Rodriguez had learned long ago and he slipped into that totally focussed mode with practised ease.

By seven that night his office looked like a bomb-site. Open textbooks and journals lay scattered over his desk and parts of the floor with relevant passages marked by bright sticky notes. Illuminated wall screens had MRI scan images on display. A white board was covered with intricate diagrams and bulletpoint plans.

He was standing in front of the white board, tapping the end of the marker against his teeth, when Layla ventured into his office.

'Thought you might like a coffee,' she said. 'And some food.'

Alex turned slowly, wondering if her presence was about to pop this comforting bubble of concentration. To his relief, the skin of the bubble appeared to be thick enough to cope. Layla was on the outside. It was like seeing her from a different perspective. Through the eyes of a surgeon and not a lover?

Whatever. He could work with that.

'Great idea.' He nodded. 'I can only stop for a minute or two, though. I think I'm on a roll with planning this surgery.'

Layla was trying to find a space to put down the carry tray that held two Styrofoam cups. She gave up and offered the tray to Alex who took one. Then she handed him a bag. 'It's nothing flashy, I'm sorry. I got one of the chefs in the cafeteria to make some filled rolls with the roast beef they had on the menu.'

'Smells good to me.' Alex unwrapped the roll and took a huge bite, letting his gaze travel back to the white board as he chewed.

Layla followed his line of vision and then turned to take in the illuminated screens. 'This looks like absolutely meticulous planning. Want to talk me through it?'

Alex shook his head. 'Later, maybe. There's one bit I haven't quite worked through yet. A bit of distraction might be helpful. Unleash my subconscious or something.' He smiled at Layla. This was working. The bubble was being protected as a private space. 'Tell me what you've been up to since I saw you visiting Tommy.'

Layla swallowed the mouthful of her own roll. She was leaning her bottom, carefully, against the edge of his desk. Alex stayed standing, too wired to sit down.

'Long meeting,' Layla told him, 'with the dieticians and kitchen management. You wouldn't believe all the stuff they've got planned for Halloween. We had to make sure that nutritional guidelines were still being adhered to and that special diets could be catered for. It meant going through every item pretty much and deciding who could and couldn't get the treats.'

'Are there going to be spiders, like you promised Tommy?'

Layla nodded happily. 'Yep. Made out of chocolate-covered marshmallows with liquorice legs and eyes. There's gingerbread cookies, too, iced to have skeletons on them. And witch's hat cookies. Upside-down cupcakes with a pretzel handle that look like brooms. Ghosts made out of strawberries dipped in white icing. I got shown pictures of what they've done in past years. It's unbelievable what a big deal Halloween is around here.'

'It's a kids' hospital. It's a big thing if they're missing out on Halloween. Wait till you see what they do for Christmas.'

'It's certainly creating a lot of excitement. Good for some kids, I guess, but Matthew was crying because he's going to go home before it happens.'

Alex nodded. Matthew was due for discharge tomorrow if everybody was happy with his progress. His speech was still slightly slurred but it was improving every day.

'I saw Felix on the ward, too. Ramona was practically chasing him down the corridor. He can crawl amazingly fast.'

'He's overdue for discharge. Nina wanted him kept as long as possible to give Ramona time to sort out her domestic stuff.'

'She said that her boyfriend was in jail, waiting for the court appearance. She's planning to take the kids back to Mexico as soon as the case is over. Her mother's arriving tomorrow.'

Alex nodded but he'd finished eating the roll now and his thoughts were drifting back to Tommy's case. He looked up at the screens. The lesion was in such a tricky place. Was he really confident of the planned route to expose it without doing too much collateral damage?

Layla's voice was soft. 'He'll be the third.'

'What?'

'Good things come in threes. Special cases this time. Felix and Matthew and...Tommy will be the third.'

'Only if I get things absolutely right. And luck's on our side.'

'The luck came when you agreed to take on the case. Nobody else could do this.'

Alex shook off the reassurance. He didn't need it. Or, rather, he did but he didn't want it to come from Layla. What if it became something he relied on, like a touchstone?

'I'm going to head home,' Layla told him then. 'You'd be more than welcome to come over when you're finished here. I don't care how late it is.'

There was a note in her voice that threatened to burst the bubble. She was offering him more than the distraction of great sex here. She was offering solace. More reassurance. The comfort of being close to someone who understood the kind of pressure he was facing. Of being *cared* for.

'Not tonight.' Alex knew he sounded curt. Knew he was pushing Layla away.

Repeating history because this was exactly what he'd done in the run-up to Jamie's surgery.

And Layla hadn't liked it. She'd wanted more attention and there'd been a showdown. Would that happen again? Would this finish, once and for all, the night before Tommy's surgery, maybe?

Alex could feel an odd prickle on the back of his neck. He had to rub at it.

But Layla seemed completely calm. She came up to him. Stood on tiptoe and planted a gentle kiss on his lips.

'I understand,' she said. 'And don't worry, Alex. I'm not going to throw some kind of hissy fit because you don't have any time or energy for me right now. It's different this time.'

The skin of his bubble was being seriously dented now. Alex pushed back, trying to restore its shape. He turned physically so that he was facing the screens and the white board. Facing his work.

'I'm not caught between a life I don't want to go back to and a future that has been taken out of reach,' Layla continued quietly. 'I think the future I want exists and that's enough for me at the moment. I'm not in any rush to get there.'

Alex had to turn back. To try and decipher exactly what Layla was saying.

Did she see *him* as part of that future she wanted?

'I know it's too soon.' Layla started gathering up the rubbish from their impromptu meal. Her movements looked jerky. Nervous, even. 'There's no pressure here, Alex. Not from me, anyway.' She looked up and caught his gaze. 'Let's just get through this week. You do whatever you need to do. I'm here if you need me but I understand completely if you don't.'

Her smile was so sweet. So genuine.

'I believe in you, Alex.'

She believed in *them*. He could see it in her eyes. Could feel the pull of it between their bodies.

He wanted so badly to submit to that pull. To burst his protective bubble himself and get so close it would feel as if they were part of the same person. Like it did when they made love. A person with the strength to get through anything. Not just to get through but to succeed. Together, they had a power that was nothing like anything he'd ever been conscious of as an individual.

But what if that connection got broken? Again?

He'd lose a lot of what he had already. The strength and power that had been painfully accumulated again piece by piece since the last time his trust in someone had been shattered.

His trust in Layla, no less.

He couldn't risk it again.

Not now. Especially not now. Who was it who said history never repeated itself? Alex had no faith in that sentiment. It only didn't repeat itself if people could stop themselves being stupid enough to step back into the same set of circumstances.

He couldn't find the words to communicate any of his thoughts to Layla. Even if he could have found the words, he wouldn't have used them because that would mean they'd talk about it and Layla would have more of those sweet, seductive words of reassurance.

And he might not be able to keep up the fight. The urge to trust those words.

To trust Layla. To imagine a future like none he had ever envisaged for himself. One that involved so much trust. Loving someone with all his heart and soul.

A family, even.

The internal struggle was fierce. He wanted it but the forces automatically there to fight back were still winning. As they always had, with the one exception of letting Layla too close back then.

So Alex didn't say anything. He nodded to show that he'd heard what Layla had said but then he simply turned back to his work. He could hear Layla behind him, quietly collecting the rest of the rubbish and letting herself out of his office.

For a moment it felt heartbreakingly lonely being by himself.

But the bubble was still intact, thank goodness, and Alex drew it more closely around himself.

The gallery was closed for Tommy Jenner's surgery.

Layla hadn't expected anything else.

It was Cade who came to find her, late in the day, to tell her that it had gone well. Even better than Alex had hoped for.

'He thinks he got it all, with a safety margin. And that any damage from the surgery will be minimal. Another course of chemo should mop up any other cancer cells that might be floating around due to the surgery.'

'Oh….' Layla felt absurdly close to tears. 'I'm so happy to hear that.' The wave of relief made her feel almost euphoric. If history really had repeated herself and the operation had been a disaster, it would have been the end of the road for her and Alex. No question about that. But now? There was hope. More than hope. Confidence almost. 'Where's Alex now?'

'In ICU. I expect he'll be there for a while yet. He won't want to leave Tommy until he's confident he's completely stable.'

Layla nodded. She could visit, though, if things were going so well. It was too big an ask to stay away for much longer. She hadn't seen Alex since she'd taken him that food in his office the other night. When he'd pushed her away and she'd said she understood.

She did. But the surgery was over now. It had gone well.

That would have changed things, surely.

It certainly seemed to have, on first glance, when Layla made her way to the intensive care unit an hour or two later. There was a quiet satisfaction to Alex's body language as he stood there, scanning the information various monitors were producing. When he looked up to acknowledge Layla, she could see a gleam of relief in his eyes.

Mike was there. Looking absolutely shattered but peaceful, sitting very still beside his son. Tommy was in an induced coma and still on a ventilator. He would be kept like that for a day or two at least, to allow his doctors to control the potentially damaging pressure that any swelling of the brain tissues could produce. His head was heavily bandaged and he was surrounded by an impressive bank of high-tech monitors that could reveal what his blood pressure was beat by beat. And what the pressures were inside his small skull. Whether his kidneys were functioning normally and exactly what percentage of oxygen he was taking in.

Life support.

The bridge between winning and losing the kind of battle that Alex, and Layla, and all the other staff here at Angel's had dedicated their lives to fighting.

Layla didn't stay long. She didn't say anything directly to Alex either, but as she left, she touched his arm. And when he looked at her she hoped she was conveying that she was with him every step of the way. That there might still be a way to go but even getting this far was a triumph that Alex should be very proud of.

He had done it.

Against some very heavy odds, Tommy had made

it through the most complex surgery Alex had ever attempted.

Well…ever since Jamie's surgery, anyway.

And so far so good. By the time Alex finally left the ICU just before midnight, with strict instructions to the staff to call him if the slightest thing changed overnight, everything was looking as good as he could have possibly hoped for.

There was more than professional satisfaction to be found right now. Something almost like euphoria was trickling through Alex's veins as he strode through the lobby and out into the night. He had no intention of going home. He'd find something to eat and then use an on-call room to grab a few hours' sleep before he went back to check on Tommy again.

He needed to get out for a little while, though. To walk off this excess of energy. To come to terms with what had to have been the hardest day of his working life. Nobody could know just how hard it had been to pick up that scalpel and begin a surgery that had, at best, a fifty per cent chance of his patient being alive by the end of it.

Not that other surgeons didn't face that kind of difficult surgery but they hadn't been through what he'd been through in the wake of the Kirkpatrick case. The public disgrace of being accused of malpractice. Of being a failure. Of knowing that his career—the most important thing in his life—was hanging in the balance and could be totally destroyed.

Nobody could understand how big this was for him. Knowing that he'd done it. More than succeeded, because he'd exorcised a ghost that had threatened to haunt him for the rest of his life.

No. That wasn't quite true.

There was one person who could understand.

The person who knew him better than anyone else alive. The person who believed in him. Who was intimately acquainted with his demons and *still* believed in him.

Alex raised his hand and flagged down a cab, which wasn't hard at this time of night. He didn't give the driver his own address, however. He asked to be taken to Layla's apartment.

Would she be there? Would she understand that there was only one way that Alex could release the huge feelings that were choking him? That some of those feelings inextricably linked to the Kirkpatrick case were also about *her* and if he'd dealt with one of those ghosts today, he had to see what it meant in relation to the other one because…because it was so big. It felt like the picture of his future was changing. Getting brighter. But he couldn't separate those ghosts so it was also confusing.

And he felt wired. Would she understand that he felt proud and excited and incredibly nervous all at the same time?

He couldn't explain why, despite the huge success of today, he felt more vulnerable than he ever had, even as a child.

Would she understand that he just needed to be with her?

Layla hadn't expected to see Alex tonight, of all nights.

She had thought he wouldn't be able to tear himself away from the intensive care unit and the watch over Tommy. That if he needed a rest he would go no further than a nearby on-call room where he could put his head down for an hour or two.

But here he was. On her doorstep. Still wearing his scrubs, as though he hadn't had the head room to give what he was wearing a single thought. Looking...

Like she'd never seen him ever look.

As if every defence he'd ever perfected had been stripped away. He looked like...Alex. Pure Alex. As if his soul had seeped into his skin and filled his eyes.

Layla felt her heart split wide open.

And the crack was big enough to gather Alex in and wrap her heart around him.

So she didn't say anything at all in greeting. She merely opened her arms as well as her heart.

And Alex stepped right inside.

Layla's bed was rumpled because she'd got out of it to answer the tap on her door. She was wearing nothing more than silk boxer shorts and a camisole top and the scraps of clothing seemed to evaporate as easily as Alex's loose theatre gear.

The sex was as different as the way Alex had looked.

Fierce and urgent but so tender it broke her heart all over again.

There was no conversation between them at all but how many times had Alex said her name?

With the groan of desire as his lips covered hers. The almost reverent whisper as his hands stroked her clothing away. The cry of need as he entered her. The echo of something she couldn't define at the moment of ultimate satisfaction. And a whisper again, as they lay, still joined, waiting for their breathing to slow and their heart rates to get somewhere close to normal again.

A whisper that could have been the start of being

able to talk but the intimate sound was drowned by the strident notes of Alex's pager.

He ripped himself away from Layla and was out of the bed in the same fluid motion.

'Rodriguez.' The greeting was almost a bark. He listened for only a few seconds. 'I'm on my way.'

And then he was pulling the scrubs back on and it took only seconds.

'What is it?' Layla had to ask, because Alex wasn't telling her. She felt like she was suddenly on another planet and the contrast to where they'd been such a short time ago was brutal.

This felt...like she didn't exist for Alex right now. Like she was back in that scary place right before Jamie's surgery. When she couldn't go back to her past life but the future she'd been dreaming of seemed to have been suddenly taken away.

No. She could cope with this. She could see the bigger picture. She could make allowances for this intense focus that had nothing to do with her.

'It's Tommy, isn't it?'

A terse nod from Alex. 'He's had a seizure.' The words were heavy. 'Intracranial pressure has spiked.'

There was nothing more to say. A headline proclaiming potential disaster and they were both too far away to gather any more information.

Layla heard her front door closing. She even heard Alex's shout seconds later as he demanded an urgent response from a cab driver.

The shivering started then. Hunched on her bed, Layla pulled the covers up to her shoulders but the chill wouldn't go away. A short time later she pushed them aside and went to find her clothes. There was no point trying to sleep so she may as well go into Angel's and find out for herself what was happening.

And it was then that the curious way Alex had said her name in that most unguarded moment came back to haunt her.

Maybe the undertone hadn't been indefinable at all.

As it echoed in her mind now, she could hear the clear notes of something that sounded horribly like despair.

Alex fought harder than he'd ever fought before.

He juggled drugs and ventilator settings and didn't leave Tommy's side until the rise in pressure that had caused the seizure was under control. It took a long time and there were more seizures before he was happy that Tommy's condition was stable.

Happy wasn't the word, of course. This was a major setback and he could see the fear in Mike's face. In Gina's, too, because she was there by his side, clinging to his hand. Sharing this horrible vigil.

A vigil that stretched and stretched. When things had been stable for thirty-six hours, Alex decided it was time to lighten the sedation and get Tommy off the ventilator.

The drugs were tailed off and the breathing tube finally removed and everyone breathed a sigh of relief when the monitors showed that Tommy was managing to breathe on his own and his condition didn't deteriorate. Mike and Gina couldn't be prised away from his bedside now because he might wake up at any moment.

Except he didn't. Hour after hour went by and there was no flicker of returning consciousness. Tommy wasn't in an induced coma now. He was in a genuine coma and things were starting to look bleak. They looked even bleaker two days later when Tommy still lay still on his bed, totally unresponsive.

'Is he going to wake up?'

Why had Layla chosen the moment that Mike voiced his worst fear to visit the intensive care unit?

Alex shook his head slowly. 'We just don't know what's really going on. We know that the cerebral blood flow is fine now but we don't know what it was like when he was so unstable. The intracranial pressure is the same deal. His level of oxygenation is good. So are his electrolytes and fluid balance. The EEG to look for brain activity was inconclusive. There's some activity. We just don't know if it's enough. Or whether the readings were accurate. We'll run the tests again tomorrow.'

'But you must have an opinion,' Mike pressed. 'You've had so many cases like this. You're the best there is and you must have a gut feeling for how this is going to go.'

Alex had to shake his head again. 'I'm sorry, Mike, but all I can say is that I really don't know. I wish I could say something else, I really do.'

'But it's not looking good, is it?'

'No.' He had a responsibility to prepare parents for the worst possible scenario when it was looking more and more likely, didn't he? 'I'm so sorry, Mike. We have to wait and see but…' It was too hard to finish the sentence. Alex's throat felt like it was closing up.

'But don't get my hopes up?' There were tears in Mike's eyes but he was trying so hard to hold it together. He knew Alex had done and was doing the best he possibly could and there was no blame in his gaze. Just despair.

Alex could only give a terse nod. He gripped Mike's arm in a gesture of sympathy but then he had to look away.

And Layla was there, dammit. With those big, blue eyes swimming with tears.

Looking as scared and grief-stricken as Mike.

He couldn't help remembering what she'd looked like just before Tommy's surgery. When she'd told him that she believed in him.

Where was that belief now?

Gone.

She was scared. Under emotional pressure. What would happen if Tommy died? Would she snap? Had she lost her belief in a future with him along with her belief in his abilities? There was no getting away from how she'd tried to take control the last time she'd been scared like this.

Would she dump him? Again?

No. He wouldn't let that happen. Couldn't afford to, if he was going to survive.

Alex excused himself from the unit. He really, really needed some time to himself.

Why did Layla choose to follow him?

Was it fate? Giving him the chance to take at least some control of this horrible situation? A way to jump before he got pushed?

'Alex...'

'Not now, Layla.' Even now he was fighting it. Postponing the inevitable despite the fact that they were out of the unit now and there was no one else around. It might be the only opportunity to have a private conversation all day.

Layla ignored his warning. How typical was that?

'I just wanted to say I'm sorry. I…feel awful that you were with me when things started to go wrong. And…and I wanted to say…don't give up on Tommy yet. There's—'

'Don't say there's still *hope*.' Alex kept his voice low to control his sudden anger. 'You and I both know what the likely outcome is.'

Layla had tears in her eyes again. Her bottom lip trembled. That fear was back in her eyes again, too, and Alex couldn't cope with that.

'Will I see you later?' The words were a whisper.

'No.' Somehow Alex found the strength he needed. And the words. 'It's over, Layla.'

She went very, very still.

'You mean…*us*?'

A single nod but Alex couldn't meet her eyes. 'You were right.' How on earth did he manage to keep his tone so light? Conversational almost. 'All it needed was to use up the fuel.' He risked a lightning-fast touch of eye contact. 'It was a pretty good fire the other night. Unfortunate that I'd decided to take a break from my professional responsibilities but there you go. It happened. And that was when I threw the last bits of fuel on.'

He managed a longer glance this time. 'I'm sorry if it's not what you want but it's all gone as far as I'm concerned, Layla. It's *over*.'

# CHAPTER ELEVEN

IT WASN'T OVER.

It *couldn't* be.

Alex might think it was but he was having a knee-jerk reaction to an emotional situation and he was taking it out on her.

Taking it out on himself, too, but he probably didn't realise that.

It was Halloween today and Angel's was buzzing with the kind of excitement that came with a special day. It was always a bonus when you could distract sick and hurting children from the frightening circumstances they found themselves in and occasions like Halloween or Christmas were gold.

There were decorations to distract a child with when something painful or scary was about to happen to them. Treats to promise for when it was over. The anticipation of the staff parade that would build all day and would not only break the normal routine for longer-term patients but make being in hospital a special place to be.

Normally, Layla would have become enthusiastically involved. She would have found herself a great costume to wear all day and had a bag of treats she could distribute to small, excited children. She'd thought about it. Tossed up between turning herself into a cowgirl to amuse the children or a witch to amuse the staff, but any incentive to play had been lost in the awful tension of Tommy's case.

And it had gone out the window completely in the wake of getting dumped by Alex four days ago.

Her secretary had been busy adding the spirit of Halloween to her office. Layla had to brush past a soft, fabric spider web hanging from her doorframe that had a very cheerful-looking plastic spider attached to its centre. A large, bright orange Jack-o'-lantern sticker on her window obscured a good percentage of the view. Not that Layla was going to be distracted by gazing at Central Park any more than by the invitations to share the fun of Halloween.

She had been so afraid that something like this might happen to destroy what she'd found with Alex. That Tommy's case was too like Jamie's not to bring the ghosts of the past out to haunt and sabotage the present. Somewhere in Alex's mind, maybe Tommy *was* Jamie. And he was bailing because he could see nothing but the rocks their relationship was doomed to flounder on.

A mirthless snort of laughter escaped Layla. It was Halloween. How appropriate that it was ghosts that were responsible for this new low point in her life.

But how *unfair*.

It shouldn't be happening because Tommy's case was *different*. Nothing had gone wrong in the surgery. There was no obvious explanation for why he wasn't waking up now. Nobody could say that Alex hadn't done everything possible. Much more than anyone else might have even attempted.

And what she and Alex had together was just as

different from what they'd had in the days of that illicit affair.

They hadn't thrown fuel onto the smouldering ashes
of what they'd had together back then. They'd started a
new fire the night they'd gone out together and talked.
They'd revealed things to each other that made them
*real* people. People with difficult, hurtful things in their
histories. They'd found a connection that went far, far
deeper than anything physical could have achieved.

She'd learned things about Alex that had shocked her
but it had also shown her how good he was at hiding
things like that. Yes, she'd been aware of the shadows
but she could never have guessed how dark they really
were. He'd had a lifetime of practice at hiding. At protecting himself from getting hurt again.

And that was what he was doing now.

Protecting himself by pushing her away, as hard and
as far as he could.

Because he didn't trust her?

Did he really think she was going to end things between them? Ever?

She'd done it once, hadn't she?

Had it ever occurred to her to wonder how much
that might have hurt him? What had happened so soon
afterwards, with the horrible publicity and the shame
of the malpractice suit had been enough of an explanation for everybody else for why Alex had been so miserable. Why he'd quit and gone to the other side of the
world, but…but what if there'd been more to it than that?
If the way she'd treated him had contributed to more
than potentially affecting his concentration the day of
Jamie's surgery?

Oh, *God*… Layla didn't think she could feel any

worse than she had been feeling for the last two days but she'd been wrong.

Sitting down at her desk, she ignored the pile of memos that would remind her of what she had to fit into today's routine. Instead, she rubbed her forehead with the base of the palms of her hands.

She'd had a premonition of precisely this, hadn't she? When Alex had walked out of Tommy's room that time and it had felt like he was walking away from *her*? That despairing note in his voice as he'd cried out her name at the climax of that extraordinary time together in the wake of the successful surgery?

She'd been so afraid of losing him.

Standing there beside Tommy's bed when Alex had been warning Mike not to hold out too much hope, Layla had seen more than the heartbreak of losing a small child. She'd seen what it would be like to lose Alex from her life and she'd been so afraid.

He'd seen that fear in her face, surely?

And yet he'd chosen that moment to run. To wall himself off emotionally so convincingly that Layla had done her best to stay out of his way. Knowing that another blow like that and what was left of her strength might desert her completely.

What would her colleagues think of their new chief of Paediatrics if they saw her sliding down the wall somewhere, to crouch in a sobbing heap, overcome by grief?

Layla raised her head. Her eyes were still closed but she took a deep, deep breath.

Not going to happen.

What was going to happen was that she would come up with a plan to take control of her own life again.

Somehow.

As soon as she could catch whatever it was that was swirling elusively around in the back of her mind.

Something that wasn't ringing true about any of this. That was adding a note of confusion.

Shining a tiny light that might feel like hope if she could just catch hold of the danged thing.

Alex was running on autopilot. There were surgeries to perform. Ward rounds to conduct. Patients to treat and parents to talk to. Any free moments he had between his duties were spent in the intensive care unit.

Checking Tommy. Going through every note that had been made. Analysing every reading any of the monitors produced. Calling experts from anywhere in the world that he could discuss the case with as he desperately tried to find an answer. A way out of this dreadful dead end.

Ryan had come into the ICU to check on one of his patients, a head trauma from a car accident earlier that day. Alex knew that underneath the theatre gown his second-in-command was wearing a pirate costume. He'd probably left his hat in his office and when he was finished here he would be heading off like everybody else to go to the ball. Halloween didn't make it into any of the intensive care units. Or into any of the operating theatres, and that suited Alex just fine.

He'd never felt less like being part of a party.

He didn't deserve to be having fun. Not when Mike and Gina were sitting here beside Tommy's bed, as pale and still as Tommy was himself. There was nothing to even talk about any more. They just had to wait. Tommy was breathing perfectly well. All his organs were func-

tioning normally. The pressure inside his skull was back
to what it should be.

He just wouldn't wake up.

And maybe he never would.

Like part of *him* never would again either. A big part.

He'd told Layla that the fire was out and there was
no more fuel to put on it. What a lie. How could you put
out a fire that was actually burning in every cell of your
body? If you did put it out, something vital would die.

Right now that part of him was in a coma. Like
Tommy. And what he didn't know was what would happen if it did die. Was it a part of himself he couldn't
live without?

Would he be on autopilot for the rest of his life?

The thought was unbearably bleak. It was a relief
to feel a tap on his shoulder and Alex turned, expecting to see Ryan.

But it wasn't. Cade had come into the ICU at some
point as he'd sat here at the nurses' station, poring over
Tommy's case notes.

'You need to get out of here for a while, man.'

Alex shrugged. There was nowhere to go. He wasn't
on call and the day's duties were long finished with.
He didn't want to go home because he'd be faced with
an apartment that was filled with memories of Layla's
company. A bed that tortured him with its emptiness.

'Come with me,' Cade suggested.

To shoot hoops? Alex shook his head. He wasn't
angry or wired enough for that to be an attractive di-
version. He'd never felt so tired in his life. So…sad.

'I've got your costume. Come and be someone else
for an hour or two.'

Now that was an attractive option. But a costume

wasn't going to make it happen. Heading off to a new job or a new country, like Cade was about to, wasn't going to fix this either. Alex had already been there and done that. He had several T-shirts, come to think of it. And look at him now. Back to square one. Trying to figure out how he was going to get through the aftermath of a case going horribly wrong.

Of getting involved with Layla Woods.

'You have to come,' Cade said. 'It's my last night here. Might be the last time we get to have some time together for a while.' His hand gripped Alex's shoulder. 'There's nothing more you can do here for now and it'd mean a lot to me, bro.'

Alex closed the case notes. He looked over at Tommy's cubicle. A nurse was hovering, probably moistening the little boy's lips or adjusting his pillow or something. Gina had her head on Mike's shoulder and he had his arm wrapped tightly around her. His other arm was outstretched, his hand completely enclosing one of Tommy's. Cade was right. There *was* nothing more he could do here. Was he getting too emotionally involved with one of his patients? Like he'd accused Layla of being so often?

And then Alex looked up and caught the expression in his brother's face. Cade was leaving a lot behind him here as he gave up his position at Angel's to head for new horizons in Australia. Bad stuff, for sure, but he was also giving up the only family he had. For a moment he looked like the kid brother Alex had let down so badly in the past.

Stiffly, Alex pushed himself to his feet.

'OK. Just for an hour or two. And I'm not saying

yes to the costume if it turns out to be the back end of a cow.'

'No.' Cade's face lit up. 'Jack Carter helped me choose. You'll love it, man. Come on, we can get changed in your office.'

New York Children's Hospital was so quiet tonight.

Everybody who possibly could go had gone to the huge fundraising ball in the nearby venue.

Not Layla, however.

She'd come to the intensive care unit to share the vigil that Mike and Gina were keeping at Tommy's bedside. Just for a while. To let them know they weren't alone. That other people cared.

Their whispered conversation had died some time ago. Now they were all sitting in a silence that was broken only by the soft beeping of the machines watching over Tommy.

Layla's thoughts inevitably turned inwards again. She was still trying to catch that elusive thought glowing, tantalisingly, just out of reach. Her gaze was on Tommy's face but she wasn't really seeing him or thinking about him. There was just a background sadness that a such a young, much-loved child could be in such a situation. Children were so vulnerable. So *trusting*...

That was it.

Layla dipped her head, closed her eyes and held her breath as she finally caught the thought. It was the way Alex had looked when she'd opened her door the other night. When she'd been able to see everything that was Alex Rodriguez. Everything about the man that she'd wanted to wrap her heart around. To love.

Had she seen the brilliant surgeon? The breathtakingly gorgeous man that turned every female head? Yes, of course, she had.

But she could see past that as well. To a frightened, lonely child who was afraid to love because people that he should have been able to trust had hurt him.

He hadn't even been trying to hide anything at all.

And that had to mean that he *did* trust her. Or could. Maybe all he needed was reassurance but what had Layla done when he'd told her it was over? Stayed out of his way. Like she had after Jamie had died because she'd felt so guilty and hadn't known what to say.

Well…she knew what to say this time.

And she'd been right. That elusive thought offered hope.

Letting her breath out slowly, Layla opened her eyes to find herself looking at Mike. And, weirdly, the warmth of hope that was seeping through her veins like a potent drug to reach every cell in her body seemed to be contagious. Mike still looked completely exhausted but his chin wasn't on his chest any more. He was looking straight ahead and he looked completely stunned. Blinded almost.

Gina had caught it, too. Her mouth was open and she was also staring straight ahead.

At Tommy? What were they looking at?

Very slowly, Layla turned her own head. Her heart missed a beat and then thumped so loudly she could swear she heard it.

Tommy's eyes were *open*.

The little boy blinked. Once…twice. His mouth opened and then closed. And then it opened again.

'Dad?' The whisper was a hoarse croak. 'Is it over now?'

Mike's outward breath was a barely controlled sob. He had to fight for control as he leaned down to kiss Tommy.

'Yes, buddy. It's over now.'

Staff came running as the monitors tripped alarms due to the unexpected increase in activity. Layla helped with the initial assessment but just as his coma had been inexplicable so was this return to consciousness. He was still very drowsy but could be roused easily now. There was no sign that he might slip back into the coma.

'Somebody needs to find Rodriguez,' one of the ICU doctors said. 'He'll want to know about this.'

'I'll page him,' a nurse offered. But she came back a short time later and shook her head. 'He's not answering his pager or his mobile. Apparently he left word that he was going to the ball for a while but would still be able to be contacted. I guess he can't hear his phone.'

'I know where it is.' Layla was already heading for the door. 'I'll find him.'

The venue was within walking distance and Layla got there within minutes. She couldn't wait to find Alex. To tell him about Tommy, of course, but more than that. Much more than that, she had to find out if the hope she was feeling about her future had a real basis. If Alex could trust her.

Could love her as much as she knew she loved him.

She entered the huge space through a doorway draped with black curtains and guarded by ghosts that had been made by white sheets draped over helium balloons so that they floated convincingly overhead. It was only then that she realised that it wasn't going to be easy to locate Alex .

There were hundreds of people here and she couldn't even see anybody she recognised because they were all disguised in an astonishing array of costumes. Not only that, the only lighting was coming from Jack-o'-lanterns on the tables and the music was loud.

Layla stood still for a minute or two, getting accustomed to this very odd atmosphere. There were groups of people standing talking, lots of people dancing and some were grouped around tables that had black coverings cluttered with wineglasses and platters of snack food. She could see ghosts and devils, clowns and fairies, a Frankenstein and a skeleton. An extraordinary couple dressed as Adam and Eve walked past her, wearing pink skin-tight body suits with fig leaves attached in appropriate places.

'Wow,' Eve shouted with laughter. 'You've come as a doctor. Very cool.'

It took Layla a moment to click and then she groaned aloud. She'd rushed out of Angel's so fast on her quest to find Alex that she hadn't bothered to take off her white coat. In this dim lighting she probably stood out as much as that man in the flashy white suit who was coming towards her. He had cowboy boots on, too, and a white Stetson hat a mile wide.

'Hey, darlin'. You've come to join the party, then?'

'Ty…' It was a huge relief to recognise someone. 'Hey, you make a good Texan tycoon.'

'I'm just tryin' it on for size. Might use this for my weddin' outfit. You'll be coming, won't you?'

'Of course I will. Have you seen Alex tonight? I'm trying to find him.'

'Who's he come as?'

'He doesn't do dress-ups.' He'd said that, hadn't he?

She'd thought he was trying to tell her that what was happening between them was real.

It was. It still could be.

'I *have* to find him, Ty. It's really important.'

'I saw Ryan a while back. He might know. He's a pirate.'

'*Layla*, hi...'

Chloe looked adorable as Wilma Flintstone in her ragged-hem dress, a necklace that looked like it was made of out golf balls and a bright orange wig that matched Brad's 'Fred' costume.

'Have either of you seen Alex?'

'He's right behind you. See?'

Layla whirled round. There were three men right behind her. Dressed identically.

The three musketeers were all roughly the same height. They all had the same black trousers tucked into boots, white shirts with flowing sleeves and tabards with a Celtic cross on the front and a cape attached at the back. They all had shoulder-length, curly black wigs, huge hats with ostrich feathers in them, masks and pencil-thin moustaches.

Three peas in a pod but only one of them was looking back at Layla with an intensity she could feel right down to her bones.

'Alex...' Layla couldn't tell if he could even hear her with this background noise. 'I need to talk to you.'

'Hey, Layla.' She recognised Cade's voice. 'This is some farewell party, isn't it? Glad you could make it.'

Layla nodded. Smiled, even, but she couldn't look away from Alex.

'You don't look like you're here to party.' The third

musketeer turned out to be Jack Carter. 'Everything OK, Layla?'

'It will be.' Layla felt absurdly close to tears. 'Alex... Tommy's woken up.'

'What? *When?*' He didn't wait for a reply. Alex grabbed Layla's hand and pulled her after him, heading for the doors. Away from the crowds and crazy costumes and all the noise. Out into the night with the trees of Central Park casting huge shadows in the light from the streetlamps. They were heading back to Angel's, still hand in hand.

Suddenly Alex stopped. 'Tell me,' he commanded. 'Tell me everything.'

It took no time at all to bring Alex up to speed on Tommy. Layla expected him to take off again. To go and see for himself that what she was telling him was true.

But he didn't. He let out a long, slow breath, closed his eyes and pulled Layla into his arms to hold her very tightly.

'Thank God,' was all he said.

A car horn sounded loudly beside them and Layla could hear some ribald shouting. Even in New York it was probably an odd sight to see a musketeer embracing a doctor. Alex caught the gist of the comments and stepped back with a wry smile.

'You're lucky you're not in a stupid costume,' he said.

'I don't do dress-ups,' Layla reminded him quietly. 'I'm not into pretending to be someone that I'm not.'

She held his gaze. 'I'm not going to live a lie or follow a script. Things are different now, Alex.'

He was listening to her words but was he hearing what she was trying to tell him?

'It's not just that Tommy's woken up and he's going

to be OK that I had to come and find you tonight. I know you think you can't trust me because of what I did last time but things *are* different now.'

Alex was still holding her hands. Did that mean something good?

'I'm not trapped any more. I'm not in a marriage that was never right. I'm not feeling guilty or scared. I'm free and I get to choose what I want and…and I want *you*, Alex. I…I love you.'

He was staring down at her. Frowning. 'But you *were* scared. I could see it when Mike was asking about Tommy. You looked like…you'd stopped believing in me.'

Layla shook her head sharply. 'Yes, I was scared. Scared of losing *you*. I can't imagine my life without you in it now.'

She still believed in him.

She *loved* him?

The news about Tommy was a huge relief but this… this was way bigger. So big that words had deserted Alex. It was Layla who broke the new silence between them.

'I thought you didn't do dress-ups, either.'

'I don't.' Alex wanted to rip the hat and wig off his head but that would mean letting go of Layla's hands. 'I thought I wanted to be someone else for a while, that's all.'

'Oh…' She understood that he'd wanted to step out of his own skin to get away from everything that was happening in his life. He could see the fear in her eyes again. Fear that she really was going to lose him?

'But I was wrong.' The words came easily now. From

a place deep inside his heart. 'I don't want to be anyone else. Not even for a minute.'

'Because of Tommy?'

'No. Because of *you*.' Alex dipped his head so that he could kiss her and the soft, welcoming touch of her lips was all he needed to know that this was right. So right it felt like he'd been waiting his whole life for this moment. 'I love *you*, Layla. I always have. And if I was someone else I wouldn't have you in my life, and I'm not going to waste another single minute of that.'

'There's a lot of minutes in every day.' Layla was smiling. 'And in every night. Can we go and visit Tommy now and then maybe go home?'

'Oh, yeah...' But Alex didn't want to move quite yet. 'How many minutes in a week are there? In a month? In a *year*?'

'Not enough, I reckon.'

Alex had an odd lump in his throat. 'Would a lifetime of minutes be enough?'

Oh...he could drown in those eyes. In the love he could see. A love that he wanted to claim. To return. For ever.

'Marry me,' he whispered. 'Please?'

It seemed to be Layla's turn to be lost for words. But she was nodding. And crying?

Layla Woods didn't cry. Unless...

She was scrubbing her tears away. 'Don't mind me,' she told him. 'I'm just so happy...as happy as a clam at high tide. Yes, Alex. I would love to marry you. As long as you don't wear that outfit to our wedding.'

'I won't, I promise.'

'Or a white suit.'

'It's a deal.'

Laughing, and still hand in hand, Alex and Layla set off again. Walking towards Angel's.

Towards their future.

\* \* \* \* \*

## *Mills & Boon® Hardback*
## *June 2013*

# ROMANCE

# MEDICAL

0513 GEN STD HB

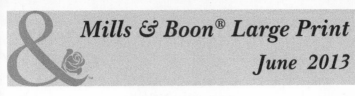

# Mills & Boon® Large Print
## June 2013

# ROMANCE

| | |
|---|---|
| **Sold to the Enemy** | Sarah Morgan |
| **Uncovering the Silveri Secret** | Melanie Milburne |
| **Bartering Her Innocence** | Trish Morey |
| **Dealing Her Final Card** | Jennie Lucas |
| **In the Heat of the Spotlight** | Kate Hewitt |
| **No More Sweet Surrender** | Caitlin Crews |
| **Pride After Her Fall** | Lucy Ellis |
| **Her Rocky Mountain Protector** | Patricia Thayer |
| **The Billionaire's Baby SOS** | Susan Meier |
| **Baby out of the Blue** | Rebecca Winters |
| **Ballroom to Bride and Groom** | Kate Hardy |

# HISTORICAL

| | |
|---|---|
| **Never Trust a Rake** | Annie Burrows |
| **Dicing with the Dangerous Lord** | Margaret McPhee |
| **Haunted by the Earl's Touch** | Ann Lethbridge |
| **The Last de Burgh** | Deborah Simmons |
| **A Daring Liaison** | Gail Ranstrom |

# MEDICAL

| | |
|---|---|
| **From Christmas to Eternity** | Caroline Anderson |
| **Her Little Spanish Secret** | Laura Iding |
| **Christmas with Dr Delicious** | Sue MacKay |
| **One Night That Changed Everything** | Tina Beckett |
| **Christmas Where She Belongs** | Meredith Webber |
| **His Bride in Paradise** | Joanna Neil |

13 GEN STD LP

## *Mills & Boon® Hardback*
## *July 2013*

# ROMANCE

His Most Exquisite Conquest — Emma Darcy
One Night Heir — Lucy Monroe
His Brand of Passion — Kate Hewitt
The Return of Her Past — Lindsay Armstrong
The Couple who Fooled the World — Maisey Yates
Proof of Their Sin — Dani Collins
In Petrakis's Power — Maggie Cox
A Shadow of Guilt — Abby Green
Once is Never Enough — Mira Lyn Kelly
The Unexpected Wedding Guest — Aimee Carson
A Cowboy To Come Home To — Donna Alward
How to Melt a Frozen Heart — Cara Colter
The Cattleman's Ready-Made Family — Michelle Douglas
Rancher to the Rescue — Jennifer Faye
What the Paparazzi Didn't See — Nicola Marsh
My Boyfriend and Other Enemies — Nikki Logan
The Gift of a Child — Sue MacKay
How to Resist a Heartbreaker — Louisa George

# MEDICAL

Dr Dark and Far-Too Delicious — Carol Marinelli
Secrets of a Career Girl — Carol Marinelli
A Date with the Ice Princess — Kate Hardy
The Rebel Who Loved Her — Jennifer Taylor

# *Mills & Boon® Large Print*
## *July 2013*

## ROMANCE

| | |
|---|---|
| Playing the Dutiful Wife | Carol Marinelli |
| The Fallen Greek Bride | Jane Porter |
| A Scandal, a Secret, a Baby | Sharon Kendrick |
| The Notorious Gabriel Diaz | Cathy Williams |
| A Reputation For Revenge | Jennie Lucas |
| Captive in the Spotlight | Annie West |
| Taming the Last Acosta | Susan Stephens |
| Guardian to the Heiress | Margaret Way |
| Little Cowgirl on His Doorstep | Donna Alward |
| Mission: Soldier to Daddy | Soraya Lane |
| Winning Back His Wife | Melissa McClone |

## HISTORICAL

| | |
|---|---|
| The Accidental Prince | Michelle Willingham |
| The Rake to Ruin Her | Julia Justiss |
| The Outrageous Belle Marchmain | Lucy Ashford |
| Taken by the Border Rebel | Blythe Gifford |
| Unmasking Miss Lacey | Isabelle Goddard |

## MEDICAL

| | |
|---|---|
| The Surgeon's Doorstep Baby | Marion Lennox |
| Dare She Dream of Forever? | Lucy Clark |
| Craving Her Soldier's Touch | Wendy S. Marcus |
| Secrets of a Shy Socialite | Wendy S. Marcus |
| Breaking the Playboy's Rules | Emily Forbes |
| Hot-Shot Doc Comes to Town | Susan Carlisle |